Trip of Terror.

Tiptoeing softly the boys made their way toward the glimmering brick passageway. The light at the far end grew brighter, and they could see the little red-and-green trolley car sitting on its rusty tracks. The shadow of the head bobbed behind the dusty windows, and in an instant the boys knew that their worst fears were true. The professor was getting ready to take the trolley on a trip back through time.

As they stood motionless, watching, an electrical hum filled the tunnel. There wasn't time to decide what to do. Both boys bolted forward and ran toward the little gilded balcony on the rear of the car. The humming rose to an ear-splitting screech as the boys clattered up the metal steps and threw themselves, facedown, on the ridged steel platform. The trolley lurched forward, and Johnny clutched frantically at the floor, trying to get a handhold. A babble of confused voices filled his ears, and he felt as if his body was turning to sand, falling to pieces. Oh, no . . . *he kept saying, over and over, but the roaring, jolting ride went on. . . .*

DISCOVER THE TERRIFYING WORLD OF JOHN BELLAIRS!

Lewis Barnavelt Mysteries

The House With a Clock in Its Walls

The Figure in the Shadows

The Letter, the Witch, and the Ring

The Ghost in the Mirror

The Vengeance of the Witch-Finder

The Doom of the Haunted Opera

Johnny Dixon Mysteries

The Curse of the Blue Figurine

The Mummy, the Will, and the Crypt

The Secret of the Underground Room

The Spell of the Sorcerer's Skull

The Drum, the Doll, and the Zombie

The Revenge of the Wizard's Ghost

The Eyes of the Killer Robot

The Trolley to Yesterday

Anthony Monday Mysteries

The Dark Secret of Weatherend

The Treasure of Alpheus Winterborn

The Mansion in the Mist

THE TROLLEY TO YESTERDAY

JOHN BELLAIRS

Frontispiece and map
by Edward Gorey

PUFFIN BOOKS

PUFFIN BOOKS
Published by the Penguin Group
Penguin Putnam Inc., 375 Hudson Street, New York, New York 10014, U.S.A.
Penguin Books Ltd, 27 Wrights Lane, London W8 5TZ, England
Penguin Books Australia Ltd, Ringwood, Victoria, Australia
Penguin Books Canada Ltd, 10 Alcorn Avenue, Toronto, Ontario, Canada M4V 3B2
Penguin Books (N.Z.) Ltd, 182-190 Wairau Road, Auckland 10, New Zealand

Penguin Books Ltd, Registered Offices: Harmondsworth, Middlesex, England

First published in the United States of America by Dial Books for Young Readers, a division of Penguin Books USA Inc., 1989
Published simultaneously in Canada by Fitzhenry & Whiteside Limited, Toronto
Published in Puffin Books, 1998

3 5 7 9 10 8 6 4 2

THE LIBRARY OF CONGRESS HAS CATALOGED THE DIAL EDITION AS FOLLOWS:
Bellairs, John.
The trolley to yesterday.
Summary: Johnny Dixon and Professor Childermass discover a trolley, which transports them back to Constantinople in 1453 as the Turks are invading the Byzantine Empire.
[1. Space and time—Fiction. 2. Byzantine Empire—History—Constantine XI Dragases, 1448–1453—Fiction.] I. Title.
PZ7.B413Tro 1989 [Fic] 88-7113
ISBN 0-8037-0581-6 ISBN 0-8037-0582-4 (lib. bdg.)

Puffin Books ISBN 0-14-130092-2

Printed in the United States of America

For Richard, Beth, and Toby—
nobody succeeds without help.

The Trolley to Yesterday

CHAPTER ONE

For a long time Johnny Dixon had been worried about the professor. The old man was in his seventies, and he had always been a bit peculiar, but lately he had been doing a lot of very strange things, and Johnny was afraid that he was losing his mind. Johnny cared about Professor Childermass a lot.

Johnny lived with his grandfather and grandmother in the town of Duston Heights, Massachusetts, and the professor lived across the street in a big, gloomy, gray stucco house. The thirteen-year-old boy and the old man were an odd-looking pair—Johnny was blond and shy, and he wore glasses; the professor was short and bespectacled, with muttonchop whiskers and a nose that looked like an overripe strawberry. But somehow they had gotten to be friends. They played chess and talked to each other a lot about history and politics and life in general. But lately things had been different.

He's acting weird. That was the thought that kept running through Johnny's mind. The professor's acting weird. Johnny was a bit on the weird side himself, and he knew it: Other kids were always making fun of him because he was lousy at sports and good at schoolwork. He was used to being an odd creature, and so was the professor. But these days the professor's oddity was something different—he just wasn't acting like himself. Usually the professor invited Johnny over to his house two or three times a week. But lately the old man had been keeping to himself. He didn't go out much anymore, except to teach his classes at Haggstrum College. Now and then Johnny would see him stalking along the sidewalk with his coat collar turned up and the brim of his battered fedora pulled down. Sometimes when Johnny woke up in the middle of the night, he would look out his window and see that the lights were on in the professor's living room. The shade was always pulled, but he could see the dark shadow of the old man. Sometimes the professor sat dead still for a long time, and sometimes he paced back and forth. A few times he seemed to be talking to someone, but Johnny could not imagine who it was. The professor lived alone, and he hardly ever had houseguests. Was he talking to himself, or to some imaginary person? Johnny had always heard that it was a sign of mental illness when people started talking to themselves. It didn't look good for the professor.

Johnny felt helpless. What on earth could he do? His gramma and grampa were kindly folks, but they didn't believe in psychiatry, and anyway they really didn't think that there was anything terribly wrong with the professor. As far as they were concerned, he was not any more eccentric than he had ever been. In desperation Johnny turned to his only other friend, a smart-alecky kid named Byron Ferguson. He called Fergie one evening and told him that he was worried sick about the professor. As usual Fergie tried to laugh the whole thing off.

"So what's wrong with the old coot?" Fergie asked cheerfully. "He been chasin' cuties down the street, has he? Or does he think he's Napoleon?"

"No, it's not like that at all!" said Johnny severely. "He's . . . well, he's sitting at home a lot and talking to himself. I'm really getting worried about him. What do you think we oughta do?"

"Steal his booze," said Fergie, giggling.

Johnny was really beginning to get upset. How could Fergie be so heartless? If the professor *had* turned into an alcoholic, it was not something to make smart remarks about. "Look, Fergie," he said angrily, "if you can't do anything but crack jokes, you can just hang up. Do you want to help me or not?"

"Okay, okay!" said Fergie soothingly. "Don't get all

hot under the collar! Why don't you and I go out after school tomorrow and play flies and grounders? We'll think of somethin' to do about the old guy."

The next day was chilly and windy, a typical March day in New England. Johnny and Fergie were out at the athletic field batting balls back and forth to each other, and when the wind caught a high fly, it sometimes took it way over onto the cinder track that surrounded the field. This was the 1950's, so when Johnny batted, he often imagined that he was one of the famous bespectacled players in the American League. Sometimes he would be Earl Torgeson, the slugging first baseman of the Boston Braves, or the Red Sox center fielder Dom DiMaggio. Johnny was not naturally athletic, but with Fergie's help he had gotten to be a fairly good fly-ball hitter. Over and over he tossed the ball up, gripped, and swung. Fergie looked awkward and uncertain as he circled under high flies, but he never missed, even though he was catching them barehanded. Then it was Fergie's turn to hit, and that was not quite so much fun for Johnny: Sometimes Fergie hit hard liners that stung Johnny's hands when he caught them, and the fly balls always made him feel dizzy when he stared up at them. They batted and caught for about an hour, and then they ambled over to a bench and sat down. As soon as he had caught his breath, Johnny started in again about the professor. He wanted Fergie's help and he wanted it bad, but first he would have to convince his skeptical friend that something was really, truly wrong.

Patiently Johnny went over all the odd things that the professor had been doing and saying lately. Then he threw in a surprise, something he hadn't told Fergie about: the sand on the study floor. Johnny told him how he had gone into the professor's house one day after hammering on the door and getting no reply. He went upstairs to the study, where the professor did his work, but the old man was not there. However, on the floor of the room were little heaps and trails of sand.

Fergie listened intently to Johnny's story, and then he made a bored face and shrugged. "So what?" he said carelessly. "So what if there was sand on the crummy floor? Maybe he went out walkin' on the beach an' he forgot to empty out his shoes till he was upstairs. He's a lousy housekeeper—you know that. If his shoes were full of sand, he'd just dump 'em out on the floor an' sweep up the mess later. Well, come on—wouldn't he?"

Johnny frowned and shook his head. "That's a dumb explanation, Fergie, and you know it as well as I do. The professor hates beaches. He doesn't even go to them in the summertime, so why would he have gone to the beach in March?"

Fergie grinned. "Maybe he's collectin' sand for a sandbox, on account of he's goin' into his second childhood."

Johnny scowled and gave Fergie a very dirty look. "Oh, sure!" he said sarcastically. "I'm sure that's exactly what the explanation is! Look, Fergie, you're being a pain in the neck, and you know it. There shouldn't have been sand on the floor of the professor's study, and if we figure out why it was there, we'll know why he's acting so strange."

Fergie was still not ready to take his friend seriously. "Okay, let's go sweep up the sand!" he said with a laugh. "Then we can have it analyzed, an' maybe we'll find out that it's from the moon, so then we can wonder how the prof got himself to the moon and back."

Johnny clenched his teeth. He had to struggle to keep from telling Fergie off. Finally, when he had calmed down, he decided to change the subject. "Okay, okay, let's forget about the sand!" he said with a scornful wave of his hand. "There's something else we ought to think about. Why does the professor sit up in his living room late at night and talk to somebody who isn't there?"

Fergie sighed. "Like I told you, he's gettin' senile. I know you don't wanta believe that, but I think it's true. My grampa went senile, an' he sat in his rocker and drank eggnog an' talked a blue streak for hours at a time until he died. And he—"

"I don't care what your stupid grandfather did!" snapped Johnny angrily. "The professor does *not* come from a family that gets senile! His father and his grandfather both lived to be nearly a hundred, and neither one of them lost his marbles—at least, that's what the professor told me. So think of another explanation."

Fergie grinned mischievously. "I'm fresh out of explanations, John baby. But I've got a great idea: Let's you and me go an' hide in his house tonight, an' then we can sneak down and listen in on what he says. That way we'll be able to figure out whether he's goin' crazy or not. Whaddaya say?"

Johnny nodded helplessly. He hated sneaking and spying, but if he had to do things like that to help the professor, then he would.

That evening, around eight o'clock, Fergie showed up at Johnny's house. They did geometry problems for a while and played two games of chess, and then, when Grampa Dixon went to the kitchen to give Gramma her insulin shot, the two boys got up and tiptoed to the front door. They opened and closed it quietly, trotted quickly across the porch and down the creaky wooden steps, and then crossed the street. When they got to the professor's front door, they were surprised to find that it was locked. This was really very unusual. The professor never locked his front door even at night, and he was always saying that burglars were welcome to come in and carry away anything they wanted. So what was going on?

"That's a heck of a note!" muttered Fergie as he stared at the locked door. "All right, what are we supposed to do now?"

Johnny bit his thumbnail nervously. "I think we ought to go around and try the back door. It'll probably be locked too, but at least we tried."

Without a word Fergie followed Johnny down the steps, across the front yard, and down the muddy, potholed driveway. When they got to the back porch, the boys went up the steps very slowly, while the boards creaked and complained under their feet. Pausing on the porch rug, they were about to step forward and try the door when suddenly the kitchen light came on. The boys froze where they stood, but luckily the shade on the porch window was pulled down. As they watched, the professor's stubby shadow moved back and forth, but it was hard to tell what he was doing. The professor sat down at a table near the window and lit a cigarette. The curling shadow of smoke rose upward, and the professor's jaw wagged—he seemed to be talking to someone. The boys noticed the shadow of something that was sitting on the table a few feet from the professor's gesturing hand. It was hard to tell what the object was, but it was about the size of a water jug. Was the professor talking to a jug? It looked as if he was.

"We've got to get closer," Fergie whispered. "That window looks like it might be open just a wee little bit. Get down on your hands and knees and follow me."

Johnny did as he was told, and the two of them inched forward across the warped boards of the porch. As they got closer to the window, they heard a muttering sound, and it got steadily louder. When they were right under the windowsill, they could hear the conversation quite clearly. The professor was talking to someone with a raspy voice and a pompous, sarcastic way of speaking.

"I think we might be able to get into the Harbor of Contoscalion," said the professor as he puffed thoughtfully on his cigarette. "And the Gate of the Contoscalion will be open till the siege is actually under way. The winds in that area usually blow—"

"The winds in that area blow where they want to blow," said the raspy voice, cutting him off. "If you want my private opinion, you'll probably wind up hundreds of miles from where you want to be. The Turks will capture you and you'll end up as a galley slave. Won't that be nice?"

"Leave it to you to be optimistic!" growled the professor. He shook his finger at the shadowy form on the table. "I tell you, this plan *is* going to work! We'll get into the city and save all those people. Isn't that a wonderful thing to think about?"

"Just super-duper wowee," said the other voice. "I'll think about it every night before I go to bed. But hadn't you better ask those other two in?"

The professor jumped a little—he seemed startled. "*Other two?* What in blue blazes are you talking about?"

"I'm talking about the two boys who are crouching under the windowsill on your back porch. They've been there for some time."

The professor swore loudly and pushed his chair back. He walked to the back door and jerked it open. With a flick of his finger he turned the porch light on, and then he stepped outside. There were Johnny and Fergie down on their hands and knees. They looked very sheepish.

The professor made strangled sounds in his throat.

He opened and closed his mouth and spluttered a bit. Finally, however, he found his voice. "*You two!*" he roared. "I should have known! I should have ***known***! You're going to ruin everything!"

CHAPTER TWO

Fergie and Johnny pulled themselves to their feet. Their faces got red, and they both tried to talk at once, but the professor cut them off.

"Be quiet!" he barked. "I don't want any flimsy cooked-up explanations from you two!" He paused, and the boys braced themselves for a scolding. But it didn't come. The professor was trying very hard to look crabby and fierce, but the corners of his mouth began to twitch, and then he started to laugh. After a while he heaved a deep shuddering sigh and pulled himself together. He took off his glasses and dabbed at his eyes with a handkerchief. Meanwhile the boys glared at him. This was worse than being bawled out—they felt silly and stupid.

"I'm sorry that I laughed," said the professor as he

put his glasses back on, "but the two of you looked so idiotic crouching under my windowsill that— Oh well, I'll save my insults for some other time. You may as well come in and meet my new friend. Come on, come on! It's quite safe, and I'm not insane, in spite of what you may have thought. So for heaven's sake, come in! It's a chilly night, and I'm freezing out here!"

With bowed heads the boys followed the professor into the kitchen. The room was in its usual state of messiness. Dirty saucepans stood on the stove, and the sink was full of dishes, glasses, and cups. However, the table where the professor had been sitting was clean. On it were three things: a potted geranium, an ashtray full of cigarette butts, and a strange-looking statue about a foot and a half high. The statue was made of polished black stone, and it was shaped like a falcon. Its wings were folded at its sides, and its hooked beak and beetle-browed glare made it look crabby. On the statue's head was an odd sort of double crown with an ornamental cobra wrapped around it.

Fergie and Johnny looked around, and they even peered under the table. Who had the professor been talking to? With an amused smile the old man walked over to the table and patted the statue on the head.

"This," he said, "is my new friend. His name is Brewster, and he—"

"My name is *not* Brewster," said the statue, cutting him off. "I am Horus, the son of Isis and Osiris, and I am a god of Upper and Lower Egypt. Don't listen to anything that this elderly wreck tells you. He's as full of garbage as a disposal unit."

Fergie and Johnny were stunned. For several seconds they just stared at the statue openmouthed, but then suddenly Fergie let out a loud, braying laugh. "Hey, I know what the heck's goin' on!" he crowed, jabbing his finger at the professor. "He's been practicin' ventriloquism, an' he's been throwin' his voice at this statue here. Hey, pretty good, prof! I coulda swore—"

"I am *not* throwing my voice," said the professor huffily. "The wretched statue actually talks, because he is . . . well, who he says he is. I like to call him Brewster because he reminds me of Brewster the rooster, who is the trademark of Goebel's beer."

"Yeah, sure, sure!" sneered Fergie, glancing skeptically at the professor. "We know all about it!"

"Oh, very well!" sighed the professor as he turned to the statue. "Show them what you can do, Brewster."

"Do I have to?"

"Yes, you do."

There was a pause. Then, as the boys watched, the statue rose slowly from the table. It turned bright pink, and then it began to spin rapidly, so rapidly that it looked like a rosy blur. Finally, when it had stopped spinning, the boys saw that the statue had turned upside down and was hovering a full six inches above the tabletop.

"There!" said Brewster crankily. "And now, if you

don't mind, I shall return to my normal shade and position. This is all very undignified, and it is making my head hurt."

With a sudden flip the statue turned right side up and landed on the table with a *thunk*. Silence fell, and the boys looked at each other. Neither of them had ever seen a god of Egypt before, and they really did not know what to say to it. With a calm, self-satisfied smile, the professor sat down in the chair that was pulled up next to the table. He took a box of Balkan Sobranie cigarettes out of his pocket and lit one.

"Now then," he said placidly as he puffed, "aren't you two going to ask me where I found this charming creature? You're not? Well, then, I'll tell you: I found him in the temple of Abu Simbel in Egypt. That is why there is sand on the floor of my study, by the way. Hrmph! To continue: I arranged it so I would be there one evening in fourteen B.C., before the drifting sand had blocked up the entrance to the temple. Otherwise—"

"You *whaaaat*?" said both boys, speaking at once.

The professor grinned toothily. "Got you with that one, didn't I? I'll bet you're both wondering how I got to a temple in Egypt in the year fourteen B.C. Come on, admit it. You're stumped!"

Fergie gave the professor a dirty look. "Well, we were kind of wonderin', but we figured you'd cook up some flaky unbelievable explanation. Didn't we, John baby?"

Johnny said nothing. He was always embarrassed when

Fergie got smart-alecky with the professor, even though he knew the old man didn't mind.

The professor sighed and ground out his cigarette in the ashtray. "I can see, Byron," he said wearily, "that you really won't be satisfied until you see my little secret with your own eyes. Very well, O ye of little faith! Come with me into the depths of the basement, and all things will be made clear." He shoved his chair back and got up, but as he was about to turn away, he paused and glanced at the statue. "Are you coming along, Brewster?" he asked.

"No," said the statue in a bored tone. "I think I shall remain here. When you have been around for five thousand years, there's nothing that can really excite or surprise you anymore. Have a good time."

"Thanks," said the professor curtly, and he motioned for the boys to follow him.

Humming tunelessly the professor marched to the cellar door, and Fergie and Johnny followed him. The old man opened the door, flipped on the cellar light, and took a long-barreled flashlight from a shelf just inside the doorway.

"I have always felt that there was something odd about this house," the professor said as he started down the cellar stairs, "but I could never quite put my finger on it. You see, the man who lived here before me was a history professor like myself, and he disappeared mysteriously in the summer of 1921. When I came here to live, I found that I was having very vivid dreams about places I had never been to, like Constantinople and Madrid and Rome. In my dreams I saw those cities as they were in the Middle Ages, which is not so strange, because my specialty in history is the Middle Ages. But the dreams always seemed so lifelike, and I saw so many things that I couldn't possibly have read about, that naturally I wondered what was causing the dreams. Well recently I took apart a set of shelves in a dark corner of my basement, and behind the shelves I found a blocked-up doorway."

"A doorway?" asked Johnny wonderingly. "Where does it go?"

The professor smiled. "That, children, is what you're going to find out."

Silently Fergie and Johnny followed the professor across the uneven cement floor of the cellar. They passed the furnace and a littered tool bench, and finally came to a dark corner where a stone archway loomed. The professor shone the beam of his flashlight down a dank, moldy-smelling tunnel of mortared stones, and at the far end the boys saw another gaping black arch. Just outside the arch bricks were stacked, and a pickaxe leaned nearby.

"As you can see," said the professor as he motioned for the boys to come closer, "I have unblocked that doorway. Come with me, but I warn you: If you feel a bit queasy, there's good reason—this is the gateway to yesterday."

After a brief hesitation the boys followed the professor through the second archway. Somewhere in the gloom the professor found a switch, and when he clicked it, three bare bulbs near the ceiling came on. The boys gasped. They were standing in what looked for all the world like an old-fashioned subway station. On the right was a raised platform with a funny little wooden ticket booth, and directly before them, mounted on a pair of rusty tracks, was a green-and-red trolley car. The railing on the rear platform still glimmered faintly with gold paint, and on the side of the car was a rusting metal sign. The flaking silver letters said ALL OUR YESTERDAYS.

"Oh my gosh!" said Johnny, and his hand flew to his mouth. Then, as he looked beyond the car, his awe gave way to disappointment. The tracks ran a little way and ended at a blank wall of granite blocks.

The professor grinned. "Doesn't look like the trolley is going anywhere, does it?" he said, walking over to the car and running a finger along the dusty rail. "That, however, is where you're wrong. The man who lived here before me used the trolley to go to— but I'll tell you about that in a minute. First I just want you two to have a look around. Enjoy yourselves."

Johnny climbed into the car and walked up and down the narrow aisle. He sat on the wicker seats and tried to read the dusky advertisements that were mounted above the windows. Meanwhile Fergie vaulted onto the platform and peered into the ticket booth. He saw a roll of faded pink tickets and a conductor's metal punch. Gritty dust lay over everything, and the shells of dead insects were curled here and there on the shelf inside the booth. As the boys poked and peered, the professor hummed and lit another cigarette. He seemed to be perfectly relaxed and at home in this strange place.

Fergie turned and stared at him. "Did . . . did the guy who lived here before you build this whole shebang?" he asked in an awestruck tone.

The professor shook his head. "No," he said. "He did not. Back around 1892 there was a plan to build a subway in Duston Heights. It was a pretty crackbrained idea, because the city doesn't need such a thing, and never did. However, the contractors did build a few hundred yards of tunnel and this charming station, but after a while the money ran out and they walled up the thing and forgot about it. Later when my friend the old historian moved into this house, he knocked down the wall between his cellar and this station, and then he decided to do a few, ah, *alterations* on the trolley car."

"Alterations?" asked Fergie. "What do you mean?"

The professor looked very smug, as he always did when he knew something that others didn't know. "Come down here, Byron," he said, motioning toward the trolley car, "and I'll show you what I mean."

Fergie jumped down off the platform and followed the professor up the steel steps into the little car. They walked to the front, where they found Johnny poring over a very strange set of controls. There were brass levers and knobs and wheels, and set in the leather-covered dashboard of the car were four tiny fan-shaped windows. Over one window the word DAY was stamped in gilt letters. Another was labeled MONTH, and still another said YEAR. The farthest window on the right was labeled PLACE. All the little windows were white and blank. Mounted before the controls was a metal swivel chair upholstered in tufted black plush.

"Pretty weird, eh?" asked the professor.

"It sure is," replied Johnny. "But how does it work?"

The professor sighed and twiddled one of the brass wheels. "As you may have guessed," he said casually, "this is a time machine. It isn't a terribly good one, because old Townsend—that was his name, Aurelian Townsend—had to use the equipment that was available to him in those days: vacuum tubes, the magneto from a model-T Ford, and batteries from a Reo electric car, and the spring-wound mechanism from an old Regina Polyphon music box. Not very efficient stuff to work with, if you're trying to leap the boundaries of time and space. Luckily, however, old Townsend managed to find the Holes of Time."

Johnny was startled. "What are those?"

Fergie shrugged. "Aah, it's just something that he made up. Look, none of this is gonna work—you can bet your bottom dollar on that. He's just tryin' to take us both for a ride."

The professor turned and glared at Fergie over the top of his glasses. "I'll take you for a ride, all right!" he said through his teeth. "But it won't be the ride that you're expecting, and when you get back you'll realize that I have *not* been talking through my hat. Unless, of course, you would prefer to go upstairs and wait for us to return."

Fergie set his jaw and looked grim. "If this piece of tin is goin' anywhere," he muttered sullenly, "then I'm goin' along too. Okay, get it moving. I'll just sit and wait." He slumped into a seat and folded his arms.

The professor sighed and shook his head. Then he asked Johnny to get out of the driver's seat. Johnny did, and the professor sat down at the controls. He twirled wheels and twiddled knobs and pulled levers, and soon the fan-shaped windows were glowing yellow. They reminded Johnny of the dial on the Atwater Kent radio in his grandparents' parlor. "These holes in time," the professor went on as he adjusted a knob, "occur for no reason in certain places. One of them is in the upper story of a three-hundred-year-old house in Topsfield, Massachusetts. But since nothing interesting ever happened there, the hole is not of much use. There's another hole in a cave at the bottom of the Atlantic, about two miles deep. But you'd need a lot of fancy equipment to visit *that* hole, so I suppose we can pass it up. *A-a-and* there's another hole at the temple of Abu Simbel in Upper Egypt, and still another in the crypt of a medieval church in London. But we are not going to any of these places."

"So where *are* we going?" Fergie snapped irritably.

"Be quiet and watch!" the professor said, and he fiddled with more dials. A loud electrical humming filled the air, and the boys noticed that the air inside the car was shimmering. The windows went dark, and they seemed to be hurtling forward at a tremendous speed. The car jolted and bumped, and the boys had to cling to the nickel-plated handles that were mounted next to their seats. The professor clutched the sides of his swivel chair, which vibrated madly, and still the wild ride went on. Johnny was afraid he would get sick, and he remembered the time when he had thrown up after riding the Tilt-A-Whirl at the local fairgrounds. Still the car jolted, and the humming noise got louder. Then, with a loud, long, ear-piercing screech of metal, the car began to slow down. Outside the windows of the trolley car, endless walls of stone seemed to be hurtling past. With a shuddering bump the car stopped, and Fergie was pitched forward onto the floor.

"Ow!" he exclaimed as he picked himself up. He felt his arms and legs, but nothing seemed to be broken.

"Are you okay?" asked Johnny anxiously. He had managed to cling to his seat somehow.

Fergie winced as he felt his elbow. "Oh, yeah, I guess so. I'll live," he muttered as he turned to look at the professor, who was clutching the safety bar on the dashboard with white-knuckled hands. "Okay," Fergie added in a loud sarcastic voice, "so what do we do now?"

He was convinced that this whole ride had been a fake, and he was sure that they were still in the dank old subway tunnel where the trip had started.

Slowly the professor pulled himself to his feet. He seemed weirdly calm, and he grinned at the two boys. "Believe it or not, children," he said, "we are here. We are just outside one of the Holes of Time, and when I open the side door of the trolley, we will be able to step out into sunlight that has not shone for five hundred years. We are still in between dimensions right now, and if you like, we can just reverse the ride and go back to my basement in Duston Heights. Are you ready to step through the door or not?"

Fergie and Johnny looked at each other. They both turned pale, and it slowly dawned on them that the professor was not bluffing. Johnny swallowed hard and wiped the sweat off his forehead with his sleeve. "I . . . I'm ready to go if you are, professor," he said in a thin, shaky voice.

Fergie grimaced. He was scared, but he was not going to back down. "I'm ready too," he muttered. "Let's get moving!"

The professor walked halfway down the car and pulled a wooden lever. With a hissing sound the side door of the trolley folded open, and the boys saw a narrow stone arch, and a streak of hard, bright sunlight beyond it. All they had to do was step over the worn wooden sill and they would be . . . where? They really had no idea.

The professor stepped forward. He reached into the pocket of his smoking jacket and pulled out a small brass object about two inches long. It was shaped like a booted foot, and it looked like one of the pipe tampers that Johnny had seen in a tobacco store in Boston. Men used them to pound down the loose tobacco in the bowls of their pipes.

"This," said the professor, "is the key that we must use to pierce the veil of time. I found it in a cigar box under the driver's seat, and it was quite a while before I figured out what it was for. Without it we can't get out of the car, and we need it to get back in. Here. Let me show you what I mean." Stuffing the tamper back into his pocket, the professor threw himself at the opening that was framed by the folding doors of the trolley. *Whump*! It was like hitting a solid oak door. He stepped back, adjusted his glasses, and turned to the boys.

"You see?" he said. "Well, now just watch!" And with that he took the brass tamper out of his pocket and thrust it into the opening. The air shimmered, and a thin veil seemed to divide. The professor stepped through, and suddenly he was on the other side. He turned and motioned for the boys to follow him.

"Come on!" he said anxiously. "The door will be open for only a couple of seconds, and then I'll need to use the tamper to reopen it. Hurry!"

After a brief hesitation Fergie and Johnny tensed themselves, and then they sprang through the opening. They looked back a moment later and saw only a blank

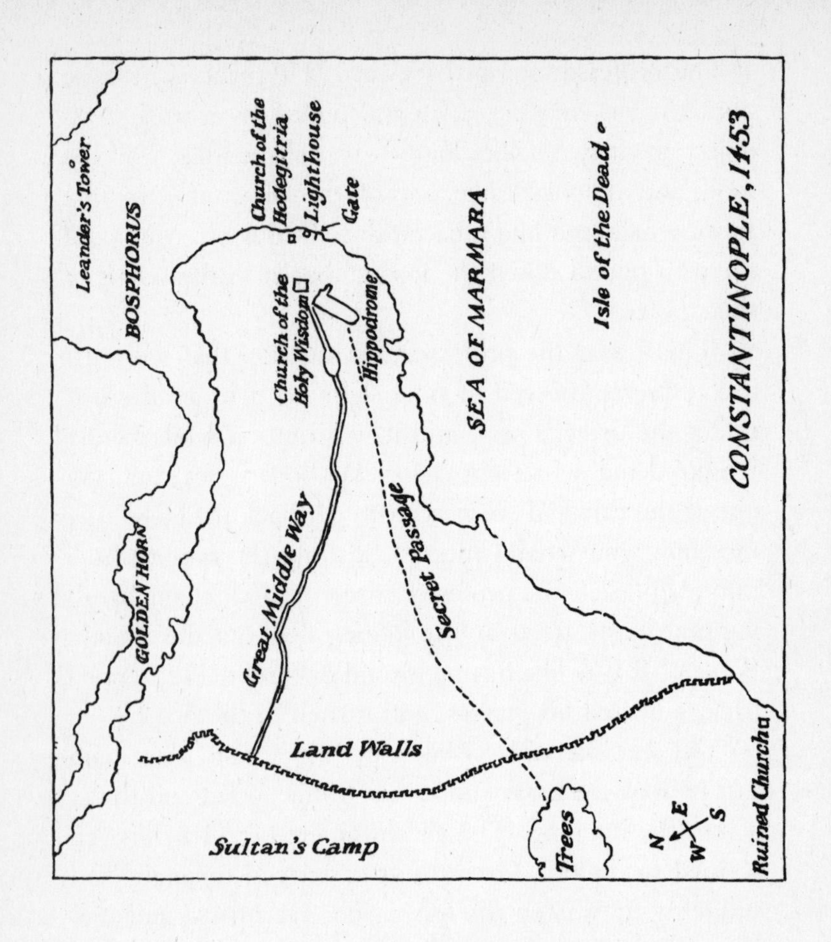

wall. Where were they? In another place and time, standing on the rough stone floor of a circular room. The walls were pierced by narrow loophole windows, and sunlight streamed in through them. Johnny ran to a window and looked out. He saw choppy, blue ocean water, and in the distance the high stone walls that guarded an ancient city. Looming beyond the walls, he saw the broad saucer-shaped dome of a large building. Johnny knew what the building was—he had seen it a thousand times in photographs that were in old books he liked to read. This was the Church of Hagia Sophia, the Church of the Holy Wisdom of God. But in the photos the old church had always been flanked by four minarets, tall towers built by the Turks after they conquered the city. Johnny saw that the towers were missing. They were not there because they had not been built yet. Johnny realized with awe that he was looking at the old city of Constantinople, where the emperors of Byzantium had ruled for a thousand years. This was not a movie set or a dream or a Viewmaster slide. It was real, and he was there.

CHAPTER THREE

For a long time Johnny, Fergie, and the professor stood looking out the windows of the stone building they were in. The walls of the city glowed golden in the sunlight, and in the distance they could see long, low ships with triangular sails cutting through the water. The city was a long way away, but Johnny thought he could see people moving back and forth on top of the walls.

"What is this place that we're in now, professor?" he asked at last. "Is it a fort or something like that?"

"Sort of," said the professor. "We're in Leander's Tower, which stands on a little spit of land in the Hellespont, the narrow body of water that runs between the Black Sea, which is north from here, and the Sea of Marmara, which is below us. Leander was a half-witted

Greek athlete who tried to swim the Hellespont so he could visit his sweetie, and he got drowned for his troubles.

"As you have probably guessed, that is Constantinople in the distance. At one time Constantinople was the capital of the great Byzantine Empire. But for centuries the enemies of Byzantium have been chipping away at the empire, conquering bits and pieces, till now there isn't much left except for the city you're looking at. The Turks have taken away just about everything that the Byzantine emperors once ruled, but are they satisfied? Not by a long shot! They want Constantinople, and they are going to fight hard to get it."

The professor paused and gazed sadly out the window. "For the time being we're here on March 30, 1453," he went on, "so the city is secure, but later a great Turkish army will arrive outside the walls. And they will bring with them a huge cannon that will batter at the ancient, crumbling stones until the soldiers of the Turkish Sultan can pour into the city and kill and loot to their hearts' content." The professor paused again. The back of his neck was getting red, and he was breathing heavily. It was obvious that he was really getting worked up.

"There will be a great slaughter in the city," he went on in a choked, emotional voice, "but the worst thing will happen in that great domed church that you see over there. On the evening of May 28, hundreds of people will crowd into the Church of the Holy Wisdom, hoping that God will protect them from the enemy. There is a legend that says an Angel of Light will come down into the church and blind the foes and drive them away." The professor's lips curled into a bitter sarcastic frown. "Silly people!" he said. "They're silly to think that an angel would protect them from a brutal enemy! No angel came, and the Turks battered down the bronze doors of the church and murdered a lot of people. The rest were taken away to be sold as slaves."

The professor bowed his head. Tears were streaming down his face, and he was biting his lip angrily. Finally he pulled himself together. He closed his eyes, clenched his fists, and grimaced. There was a long pause, and Fergie and Johnny looked anxiously at each other.

"I'm sorry that I lost control of myself," the professor said stiffly as he stared longingly out the window. "I know it's ridiculous to get all worked up about something that happened five hundred years ago, but I've been reading about the siege of Constantinople all my life, and now here I am, about a mile and a half from the city, just before the siege begins, and . . . well, you would think I would be able to *do* something!"

Johnny blinked. "Do something? Like . . . what?"

A light had dawned in Fergie's eyes. He grinned wickedly. "Hey, I know what you could do, prof!" he said gleefully. "You could get a machine gun and get up on those walls over there, and when those crummy Turks go chargin' in, you could mow 'em down! Boy, would *they* ever be surprised!"

The professor eyed Fergie coldly. "I might have known that you would come up with a clever idea like that," he growled. "But I am not going to become a murderer. There has to be some other way!"

Fergie looked disgusted. "Like what?" he said.

"I don't know," said the professor in a low voice. "But by God I'm going to find a way. You just see if I don't!"

There was another long silence. Johnny leaned out a window. He could feel the rough stone sill under his hands, and he could smell the brackish sea air. He could see the shining walled city that looked so beautiful and dreamlike in the afternoon light. Johnny felt a sudden surge of hope in his heart. Maybe the professor could do something. Maybe he could change the course of history and drive away the Turkish army that would soon be outside the gates of Constantinople. But then Johnny was filled with despair. If the professor would not use modern weapons of destruction, how could he defeat the Turks? He couldn't chase them away with a broom, or with Halloween masks, could he? But maybe . . .

The professor's voice interrupted Johnny's thoughts. "Come on, boys," he said as he pulled the pipe tamper out of his jacket pocket. "We had better be getting back to Duston Heights and the middle of the twentieth century. Your grandmother will be looking for you, John, and I'm sure Byron has homework to do. Come along."

As he followed Johnny and the old man back through the magic doorway, Fergie thought of something. "Prof?" he asked. "I hate to be a pest, but well, wouldn't the local people think it was kind of weird if they looked up and saw a trolley car hangin' outside one of the second-floor windows of their tower?"

The professor chuckled. "It would be something to stare at, wouldn't it?" he said as he sat down in front of the trolley's control panel. "However, as strange as it may seem, the car is invisible. It's invisible because it's really not *here* . . . not in the normal sense of the word. It's hanging in between dimensions, with its motor idling, waiting to go backward or forward in time. Now take your seats and grab hold of something. The Duston Heights Rocket is about to make a return trip."

Johnny and Fergie grabbed their seats, the professor twiddled with the dials and levers, and the trolley took off on a clumpy, clattering, bone-jarring ride. When it stopped, both Johnny and Fergie were pitched forward onto the floor of the car, and the professor bumped his head on the windshield. Dazed and shaken, the three of them climbed down out of the car and walked slowly to the arch that led back to the basement of the professor's house. For a long time no one said anything—the boys had been astounded by the things they had seen. Fergie's mind was racing, and he kept trying to convince himself that the whole trip had been a fake. But he had smelled the salt air and seen the sun shining on the honey-colored walls of Constantinople. If the trip was an illusion, it was a pretty good one. When Johnny's head began to clear, he remembered the things that he and Fergie had heard when they were hiding under the windowsill of the professor's back porch. Was the old man really planning to go to Constantinople and drive the Turks away? It had sounded as if he and Brewster were discussing ways of getting into the city. If that was really what was on his mind . . .

"Professor," said Johnny suddenly as they were starting up the cellar steps, "you're not really going to try to fight the Turks, are you?"

The professor jumped as if someone had stuck a pin in his arm. "Hah?" he said in an abnormally high voice. "Am I going to—" Suddenly he broke up. He laughed loudly. "What an idiotic notion! How on *earth* could an old fogey like me change the course of history? How could I possibly fight the eighty thousand soldiers that the Turkish Sultan is going to throw at the walls of Constantinople? I'm not a hero, and I certainly don't intend to get killed in a battle that was fought hundreds of years before I was born. Don't get all worked up, John! I may go back and watch the battle from Leander's Tower, but I won't risk my neck. Merciful heavens, how could you think that I would? I'm not *that* crazy!"

Johnny eyed the professor skeptically. He had known the old man for quite some time, and he could guess when he was putting up a front. Johnny couldn't very well call the professor a liar, so he just nodded and smiled. But in his heart he was alarmed, and he wondered what he could do to stop Professor Childermass if he decided to become some crazy kind of hero.

When they got back upstairs to the kitchen, Johnny and Fergie were surprised to see that Brewster was gone. The professor did not seem concerned. He merely yawned.

"I wouldn't worry if I were you," he said in a bored tone. "He's gone off to outer space or inner space or *somewhere*, but he'll be back eventually. As for me, I'm going to bed in a few minutes, but I can offer you boys some cocoa before you leave. How about it?"

Johnny and Fergie agreed, and they sat around and chatted while the professor heated up water on the stove. After drinking the cocoa, the boys left. They both felt a bit dazed, but they were happy. Happy about the wild experience they had had, and anxious to try it again sometime soon. But Johnny was still worried about the professor.

CHAPTER FOUR

The winds of March blew hard, and the boys had to lean forward and struggle sometimes as they made their way to school. Toward the end of the month Haggstrum College let out for spring vacation, and the professor went to visit his friend Dr. Charles Coote, who taught at the University of New Hampshire. Johnny was relieved because he knew that the old man was not going on a trip to Constantinople—at least, not right away. But now that his house was empty, a plan began to form inside Fergie's restless brain. One evening when he and Johnny were walking home from the movies, Fergie started to talk about his clever idea: Wouldn't it be great if the two of them could get into the professor's house and take the Time Trolley for a little jaunt? Fergie didn't want to go very far, just to Topsfield. They could visit it back in the horse-and-buggy days and spend an evening wandering around the town. Then they could zip back to Duston Heights. There was no reason the professor would ever have to know what they had done.

When Fergie had finished outlining his plan, Johnny stared at him in disbelief. He was so flabbergasted that it took him a while to find his voice. "Fergie," he said at last, "we don't know how to run that trolley. What if we get stuck back there in eighteen-something? What'll we do, go find our great-grandfathers and say, 'Excuse us, but we're due to be born in about fifty years, and we wonder if you could help us'? Come on, Fergie! Your plan is just as nutty as the one the professor dreamed up."

Fergie waved his hand scornfully. "Aaah, Dixon, you're a worrywart! You'd never have any fun if it wasn't for me. Look, all we're gonna do is zip back to the time hole in the upstairs story of that old house. The professor told me about the place. It's called the Parson Somebody house, an' it's three hundred years old an' it's a museum. Nobody lives there. We can just arrive at night an'—"

"Hey, wait just a minute!" said Johnny, interrupting. "The place is a museum *now*, but how about fifty years ago? Maybe the place'll be swarming with people. What'll we do then?"

"Punt!" said Fergie, grinning. "Dixon, I wouldn't

worry: If there's people in the house, they'll be asleep, an' we can just tiptoe on downstairs an' out the front door. Wear your tennis shoes."

The two walked on a little farther in silence. Then Johnny spoke up again. "I went into the professor's house once when he wasn't there, and I felt bad about doing it. It made me feel like a louse."

Fergie gave Johnny a shifty sidelong glance. "You've got a key to his front door. He gave you a key the other day after you complained to him about how you left your notebook in his house an' you couldn't get it."

"Yes, he gave me a key," said Johnny, frowning stubbornly, "but that's not the point. The point is—"

Fergie cut him off. "The point is you're scared an' you're making up reasons not to go. Come on, admit it!"

"I'm *not* scared," muttered Johnny through his teeth. "I'll go anywhere you go. Only—"

"Great!" said Fergie, slapping him on the back. "So how about tomorrow night?"

As the two walked on, Fergie kept wheedling and arguing. Gradually Johnny's resistance began to weaken. To tell the truth, he wanted very much to take a quick, safe trip in the Time Trolley while the professor was gone. Finally he gave in. Yes, he said, he would meet Fergie on the professor's porch tomorrow night at fifteen minutes before midnight. But they had to be very careful, and they couldn't stay very long in Topsfield, and they couldn't get into any kind of trouble. Fergie promised that it would be a problem-free trip. It would be a breeze, an absolute breeze.

On the following night, as a cold wind whistled through the bare trees on Fillmore Street, two figures crouched in the dark shadows on the professor's front porch. Both of them were wearing parkas and gloves, because they had decided to visit Topsfield in the winter. Fergie held his flashlight, but he had not turned it on yet, and he stood fidgeting impatiently as Johnny fumbled with the door key. Finally he found the hole, and the door rattled open. The two boys disappeared into the dark front hall and shut the door quietly behind them. Fergie clicked on the flashlight in his hand, and the two of them made their way down the hall to the kitchen, which led to the cellar. As he laid his hand on the cold knob of the cellar door, Johnny paused and turned to Fergie.

"Are you sure you wanta do this?" he asked in a quavering voice.

"Yeah, I'm sure!" said Fergie firmly. "Go ahead, open it."

The boys walked down the cellar stairs. When they got to the brick passageway, they felt around on the wall until they found the switch that turned on the lights in the subway tunnel. The trolley car looked like some large, expensive toy. Without a word Fergie walked to the car and trotted up the steps. Johnny swallowed hard, but after a brief pause he followed.

Fergie was seated at the control panel. He had turned on the lights inside the car, and he munched a Clark bar calmly as he set the various dials: The PLACE dial read TOPSFIELD, and the other dials twelve midnight, December 5, 1896. With quiet self-assurance he moved the lever that started the trolley's motor. As the dials glowed and the machine hummed, Fergie turned to Johnny and grinned.

"See? It's as easy as pie! Grab a seat, John baby, 'cause we are goin' on a ride! Hang on to your bridgework, everybody!"

Johnny sank down onto one of the wicker-covered seats, and he gripped a nickel-plated handle. The lights grew dim and yellowish, and the air in the car wavered and rippled. With a hiccupy lurch the car went forward. Faster and faster it sped, and endless stone walls rushed past the windows. At last the car slowed to a stop. Johnny sat dead still in his seat, and he still clung with a death grip to the safety handle. He knew they were there, but he did not want to get up and go out.

"Well, kid, we made it!" said Fergie cheerfully. He tried hard to sound carefree, but his voice was unnaturally high, and it trembled just a bit. After a quick glance at Johnny, he reached under the seat and pulled out the cigar box. When he opened it, he heaved a sigh of relief: The tamper was there.

"Okay, John baby!" said Fergie as he jumped up. "I got the magic whoopyjigger, so let's go see what's up in good old Topsfield." He paused by the side door of the trolley and glanced again at Johnny. "Hey, what's the matter? You look sick."

Johnny was sick. His face was pale, and his stomach was churning. He felt as if he was about to make a parachute jump with a lace doily for a parachute. But he gritted his teeth and forced himself to stand up. With unsteady steps he moved toward the door.

"Okay," he muttered, setting his jaw grimly. "Do your stuff!"

Fergie raised his hand and pulled the wooden handle. The doors hissed open, and they saw . . . only darkness.

Johnny peered anxiously over Fergie's shoulder. "Is . . . is something wrong?" he asked nervously. "Shouldn't we be . . . in a room or something?"

Fergie shook his head. "The prof never told us *exactly* where the time hole would be," he said. "Maybe we're in a room without any windows. Let's see."

Fergie flicked on his flashlight, and he raised the tamper. When it touched the invisible veil, the air shimmered, and Fergie stepped forward. Then, suddenly, he tripped and went sprawling. They were in a deep, narrow closet, and the floor was covered with firewood.

As he fell, Fergie's hands hit the closet door, and it flew open. Quickly he scrambled to his feet and staggered out into the room, which lay bathed in moonlight. It was a bedroom, and the boys could see the shadowy forms of a dresser, a washstand, and a fourposter bed. Curtains hung down from the side of the bed that was nearest them, and as they watched in horror, a hand twitched the curtains aside and a loud, masculine voice rang out:

"Who's there?"

Fergie thought quickly. He had managed to hang on to the flashlight, and now he raised it and held it up under his chin, so that it bathed his face in a ghastly pallor. In a deep, sepulchral voice he moaned: *"I am a restless spirit, doomed to walk the earth at the mid of night! Beware!"*

With a loud curse the man in the bed swung himself up into a sitting position. He pushed the curtains farther back and lurched to his feet. The boys saw a tall, barefooted figure in a long white nightgown and a tasseled white cap.

"Spirits, my grandmother!" the man roared angrily. *"You are a snot-nosed boy, and a burglar besides! How the devil did you get in here?"*

Fergie stood dead still; he really didn't know what to do at this point. Behind him Johnny cowered in the doorway of the firewood closet. Noiselessly he dropped to his knees and began to crawl around past Fergie's legs. So far, in the pale light, the man hadn't seen him. As the man started to yell even more loudly at Fergie, Johnny threw himself, rolling like a barrel, at the man's legs. He went down like a bowling pin, sprawled headlong across Johnny's body. In a flash Johnny was on his feet and running for the narrow staircase opening in the far corner of the room. Fergie was right behind him.

Quickly they clattered down the steps and began struggling with the heavy iron bolt that held the front door shut. The bolt resisted at first, but finally it slid back, and the two boys raced out into the cold winter night.

They ran down a shoveled path, turned, and staggered off the road into deep snow. A screen of tall fir trees hid them as they made their way across the village common. Finally, out of breath, they stopped by the corner of a two-story building with a row of flat white Grecian columns in the front.

"I . . . don't think . . . I can go . . . any farther," Johnny panted. "Is . . . is he following us?"

Fergie paused until he had his breath back. "I dunno," he said as he peered out across the moonlit common. "Hey, that was a real good rolling block you gave him. Way to go!"

Johnny smiled weakly. He had never thought that he was capable of doing a thing like that, but somehow he had managed to. As he crouched in the deep snow, he began to feel very daring and adventurous. He was about to say something when he felt Fergie grab his arm.

"Hey, look!" he whispered. "There he is!"

Sure enough a tall man in a nightgown was making his way out into the middle of the snowy common. The boys could see him pretty well in the moonlight, and they noticed that he had long sideburns and a handlebar mustache. In one hand he carried something that looked like a one-handled rolling pin. Johnny had seen a weapon like it in his grandparents' attic. It was called a life preserver, and it was weighted with a piece of lead. You could split a person's skull with a thing like that.

"All right, you boys!" yelled the man as he glared about fiercely. "I'm going to talk to the police about you in the morning! Your parents ought to be ashamed of themselves!"

Finally, after shouting a few more unpleasant remarks, the man left. When they were sure he was gone, the boys pulled themselves to their feet.

"What did he mean about our parents?" asked Johnny, brushing snow off himself. "He can't know who we are, can he?"

Fergie waved his hand scornfully. "Aah, he was just bluffin'! He was tryin' to scare us. We'll wait till he goes back to sleep, an' then . . ."

Fergie's voice trailed away. Johnny looked at him suddenly. A vague fear was growing in his mind. "Fergie," he asked timidly, "is—is something wrong?"

"Oh, not much, John baby," muttered Fergie. "Not very much! I just lost the magic pipe tamper, that's all!"

Johnny turned pale. Without the tamper they were stuck forever in 1896. This was awful, as bad as anything he could have imagined. "Oh my gosh!" Johnny gasped. "That's *terrible!* How did you lose it?"

Fergie hung his head. "I don't know," he said sullenly. "I think I must've dropped it when I fell over those logs in the closet. So it's in there, or else out on the bedroom floor somewhere. Don't worry, we'll find it."

Johnny looked at Fergie in despair. "Don't worry?" he said. "Don't *worry*? Good God, Fergie! First you tell me that the house'll be empty because it's just a museum, and now you tell me that you've lost the tamper, only we shouldn't feel bad because you'll get it back for us real quick! Am I supposed to be happy because we're gonna turn into old men and orphans in this crummy place?"

Fergie turned to Johnny, and in the moonlight his face looked strained. His lower lip began to tremble, and tears filled his eyes. "I . . . I didn't mean for it to happen," he said in a quivery voice. "I'll fix things up. It'll be all right."

Johnny's angry mood vanished. He had never seen Fergie in a weepy state before. Usually his friend was a stiff-upper-lip, tough-guy sort. Johnny just couldn't stay mad at him. Together they would figure out what to do.

Fergie clenched his fists and pulled himself together with a sigh. "We're gonna have to wait till that crab with the face lace goes to sleep. Then we'll sneak up to his bedroom and find the tamper. It's gotta be in the closet or on the floor in the room *someplace*."

There was such a sound of grim determination in Fergie's voice that Johnny felt comforted. Somehow he felt they would win out. But for the time being there was nothing for them to do but stand in the snow and wait. A freezing wind began to blow, and they both shuddered, even though they were wearing their winter coats. The corner of the building shielded them a little, but not much. The snow on the broad common sparkled in the moonlight, and a horse carriage came rattling down the road near them. The driver was hidden by the black leather hood of the carriage, and the two oil lamps mounted on the dashboard cast a wavering faint yellow light. Who was it? A doctor out on a late-night sick call? Someone up to no good? Johnny and Fergie would never know. The carriage disappeared up the road, and the moonlit silence returned. Across the way the clock in a church steeple tolled one—they had been here in 1896 for an hour.

Johnny took off his gloves and stuffed them into his coat pocket. He flexed his stiff and reddened hands. "When do you think we can go back? he asked anxiously.

Fergie scratched his nose and bit his lip. "I think it might be safe now," he said at last. "We oughta try anyway, before we freeze to death. Come on."

Silently Johnny and Fergie picked their way back across the common toward the dark house, with its overhanging second story and huge central chimney. A row of icicles hung from the eaves, and the small diamond-paned windows glimmered gray. They did not pause to test the nailstudded front door; they knew it would be locked. Instead they made their way around to the back, where, set into the stone foundation, there was a slanted double-leaved cellar door. The only thing that fastened it was a small branch shoved through the two door handles.

As carefully as he could, Fergie eased the branch out and pulled back one of the door leaves. The two boys followed stone steps down into a dark cellar that smelled of earth and mold. Fergie switched on his flashlight. They found steps that led upstairs, and at the top there was a room with a huge fireplace and a long wooden table flanked by cane-bottomed chairs. They continued toward the front of the house; they knew that the staircase to the second floor was there. Fergie turned the flashlight off, and he and Johnny crept forward on hands and knees till they reached the front door. Before them the narrow, shadowy staircase led up to the second floor. Johnny swallowed hard. What if the nasty man was squatting at the top of the steps with a pistol or a club in his hands? He paused, and so did Fergie. For a full minute they waited, listening for the slightest noise. Except for the faint sound of wind outside, all was still.

"We have to go up," Fergie whispered. "It's the only way."

Johnny nodded, and he started climbing one step at a time on hands and knees till he was peering into the moonlit room. The last red embers of a fire glowed in the fireplace. The curtains of the bed were drawn shut, and Johnny could hear a muffled snoring sound. He crawled across the floor, and Fergie followed. They stopped by the door of the firewood closet.

"Where do you think the tamper is?" asked Johnny in the faintest of whispers.

"Like I said before, I don't know," muttered Fergie.

"I hit that dumb door with my hand when I fell down. It might be anywhere in the room, or in among all those logs in that dumb closet. Just stay put and I'll look for it."

In an agony of fear Johnny crouched by the closet door while Fergie scuttled around on the worn boards, feeling here and there with his hands. He had his flashlight, but he didn't dare turn it on. To Johnny it seemed like ages were passing. At any moment the man in the bed could come charging out, and the two of them would be doomed. Fergie went on searching. Johnny turned his head, and he saw to his horror that Fergie was under the bed! Then, suddenly, Johnny heard a metallic *clack*. With a soft shuffling sound Fergie crawled back and stopped near him. He was breathing heavily, and he held up something that glimmered faintly in the moonlight.

"I found it!" he whispered. "Let's get outa here!"

But he had spoken too loudly. The bed creaked, and with a muttered curse the man awoke. His bare legs came swinging out through the curtains. The boys were on their feet, and Fergie jerked the closet door open. In they went, picking their way clumsily over the firewood, till they reached the shimmering veil. Behind them they heard the man's quick footsteps as he hurried toward the door. In a flash Fergie raised the tamper and parted the veil; the boys dived inside, and the veil closed behind them as they rolled across the metal floor of the trolley. When they picked themselves up and looked back, they saw the tall burly man staring at the outside of the veil. To him it looked like a blank wall.

Fergie thumbed his nose at the man and ran to the driver's seat. Working feverishly he set the dials for the return trip, and Johnny scarcely had time to sit down when the trolley began to hum and whine. The trip back was a bit bumpy, but they arrived safe and sound. Fergie shut off the dials and put the tamper back in its box. Then he heaved a deep, heartfelt sigh of relief.

"We made it, John-O!" he crowed with a wide grin as he slapped his friend on the back. "I told you we would, didn't I?"

Johnny took out his handkerchief and mopped his sweaty, pale face. "Fergie," he said quietly, "I don't want to do anything like this again. Do you hear? Not *ever*!"

CHAPTER FIVE

Johnny sneaked back into his house that night without being spotted. When he met Fergie after school the next day, they talked about their adventure, which was already beginning to seem like something they had dreamed. That evening the professor came back from his trip, and the boys wondered if he had noticed that anything was wrong. When they talked to him, he did not give any sign that he was upset; but the next afternoon Johnny noticed that a locksmith's truck was parked in front of the professor's house. Grampa said that the professor was having his front- and back-door locks changed. Johnny's heart sank, and the next time he visited the professor for a chess game, he braced himself for a bawling out. But none came. The professor was his usual cranky but kindly self, and he had baked a chocolate cake, which was as delicious as always. Once or twice when Johnny glanced at the old man across the chess board, he thought he saw a sly smile, as if the professor was enjoying some private joke.

A week passed, and nothing very exciting happened. Johnny got an A on an algebra test, and the kite-flying season began out at the Duston Heights athletic field. Johnny and Fergie studied together a lot, because there was a big history test coming up and half the kids in their class were scared to death of failing it. Johnny and Fergie were both pretty good at history, so they weren't really very worried, but they hit the books anyway because they enjoyed being together. Sometimes they went to the movies after they had finished doing their homework, and as they walked home they always stopped near the professor's house and looked to see if the basement light was on. Sometimes it was, and sometimes it wasn't. The professor was being more friendly these days, but he still acted secretive, and this was exasperating to the boys. Let's wait till he makes his move, Fergie said, and he said it often. At first this advice sounded good to Johnny, but gradually he began to realize that Fergie wasn't making sense. He told him so one afternoon when they were gobbling hot-fudge sundaes at Peter's Sweet Shop.

"What good is it gonna do for us to wait?" Johnny asked irritably. "If he decides to zoom off to Constantinople and save those people from the Turks, we'll never know till he's gone."

Fergie smiled knowingly and held up his dripping spoon. "Ah, that's where you're wrong, John baby!" he said. "That's where you're *wrong*! He's got to get together some equipment."

Johnny was mystified. "Equipment? What do you mean?"

Fergie's grin got wider. "I mean a gun, John baby. You didn't really believe all that stuff about how he wouldn't use a machine gun on the Turks, did you?"

Johnny could feel his face getting red. "If you really want to know, Fergie," he said angrily, "yes, I do believe what the professor says. He hates guns."

"Yeah, yeah, sure!" sneered Fergie, waving his hand scornfully at Johnny. "Look, kid. The prof is a little nutty, but he isn't all *that* . . ."

Fergie's voice trailed away. He had seen something out of the corner of his eye. The two of them were sitting in a booth near the front of the shop, and Fergie had caught sight of the professor's car through the big display window. "Hey!" he said excitedly. "Hey, John baby, look at that! The prof is goin' down the street, and I'll betcha he's goin' to the Merrimack Sporting Goods Shop to buy a rifle. How much you wanta bet?"

Johnny winced. He didn't like gambling, but Fergie had just declared war. "All right!" he said hotly. "I'll bet you fifty cents he isn't buying a gun."

"You're on!" said Fergie, and he slapped Johnny's hand to seal the bet.

The two boys finished their ice cream quickly, paid at the counter, and hurried out. The Merrimack Sporting Goods Shop was about a block and a half down the street, and they walked along slowly on the side of the street that was across from the shop, so the professor wouldn't notice them. By the time Fergie and Johnny got there, the professor had parked his car and gone in. Johnny peered at the display window that was full of shotguns, rifles, and target pistols. His heart sank, and he began to think that maybe Fergie was right. Minutes passed. The two boys crouched down behind a pickup truck and waited to see what the professor was going to bring out of the store. As the minutes ticked by on Johnny's watch, he wondered what on earth the old man was doing. Finally the professor came out, and the owner of the shop was with him. They were carrying a large yellow rubber inflatable life raft, the kind that comes with a paddle and a cylinder of compressed air, wrapped up with luggage straps.

"Oh my gosh!" whispered Fergie, and he put his hand over his face. "He's gonna try to get to Constantinople in that thing! He'll drown himself, that's for sure!"

Johnny was very alarmed. He had won his bet with Fergie, but that didn't matter to him now. What they had just seen was proof that the professor was going to try to get into the walled city. Once he was inside, what was he going to do? The boys didn't have the foggiest idea. They knew the professor wanted to save the people who were trapped inside the great Church of the Holy Wisdom, but they didn't know how. The whole idea seemed crazy and harebrained, and Johnny was afraid the old man would get himself killed or disappear forever into the past.

With the owner's help the professor lashed the rubber raft to the top of his car. As he drove off, Fergie stood up and let out a long, low whistle.

"Boy!" he said, folding his arms in disgust. "Ain't that somethin'? He's gonna go back there an' try to scare away those Turks with his Knights of Columbus sword! I really didn't think he was that wacky."

"Fergie," said Johnny in a low, serious voice, "we've got to stop him! Otherwise he'll get himself killed!"

"Relax, John baby," said Fergie soothingly. "Byron Q. Ferguson always comes up with some clever idea that will save the day."

Johnny glanced at him skeptically. "Oh, yeah? Like what?"

Fergie shrugged. "I haven't thought of it yet, but give me some time. Just give me a little bit of time, an' I'll figure out what to do."

Maybe they had time, and maybe they didn't. For all the boys knew, the professor might be planning to zoom off to Constantinople that very night. If he did, what could they do? Not much, and they knew it.

April violets sprang up as the days passed, and mild breezes blew. Every morning as he got ready for the long walk to school, Johnny glanced across the street to see if the professor was getting his car out of the garage. Usually he had eight-o'clock classes at Haggstrum College, and if he wasn't in too big a hurry, he would offer Johnny a ride. On mornings when he saw the car backing out, Johnny heaved a sigh of relief. Bu if the car stayed in the garage, he fussed and fretted. Was the professor in his house, or had he gone back to a world of long ago to carry out an impossible plan? By the time a week had passed, Johnny was convinced that the professor would be making his move soon. He and Fergie had better get busy and figure out a way to stop him.

One cold, drizzly evening toward the middle of April, Johnny and Fergie were playing chess in the parlor of the Dixons' house. They sat at a table that was drawn up near the big bay window, and they were both having a lot of trouble keeping their minds on the game. Every now and then one of them would glance quickly at the dark house across the street. There was a light on in the study window upstairs. That probably meant that the professor was grading papers. Unless, of course, he had left a light on up there to confuse them while he was poking around in the dark down in the cellar. The lights in the old subway tunnel couldn't be seen from outside, so he could be getting ready to go, for all they knew.

Johnny moved a bishop and then peered again out the window. When Fergie saw the move his friend had made, he laughed.

"Come on, John-O, give it up!" he said as he shoved

Johnny's king over onto its side. "You're not payin' any attention to this game, and neither am I! We oughta just go over there and hammer on his door an' yell *Hey prof, what's up?* or somethin' like that."

Johnny grimaced. "Oh, sure!" he said sourly. "That'd be just an A-number-one fine idea! We wouldn't get anywhere if we did that. He'd just pretend that he didn't know what we were talking about. Or else he'd give us that routine about how he just goes to the tower to stand and look at the city. If he ever does try to save those people in Constantinople, he'll go at three A.M., and we'll never know anything about it till he gets back—if he does get back."

Fergie set his jaw—he looked grim and determined. "I hate to admit it, but I think you're right," he muttered. "So I guess there's only one thing to do—we have to fix it so the prof can't leave the tower." With a wicked grin Fergie reached into his hip pocket and pulled out a switchblade knife with a black bone handle. He touched a button, and a long glittering blade flew out with a snicking sound.

Johnny was stunned. Fergie often dressed like a leather-jacket hood, but he had never carried a knife before—not as far as Johnny knew, anyway. "Fergie!" he whispered in a shocked voice. "For gosh sakes, put that thing away! If my gramma sees you with that, she'll toss you out on your ear! Why did you bring *that* along?"

With a frown Fergie folded the knife up and stuck it back in his pocket. "Don't get yourself in an uproar,

John baby," he said softly. "I just wanta use this thing to cut some nice big holes in the prof's raft, so he can't use it. Doesn't that seem like a good idea to you?"

Johnny thought for a bit. "Yeah, I guess so," he said slowly.

"But what if he takes the raft out in the water and it sinks under him and he drowns? How do you think we'll feel then?"

Fergie grinned maliciously. "Aah, he'll never get to the water with *that* raft! I'm gonna cut so many holes in it that it'll look like a big yellow Swiss cheese. He'll just have to climb into the trolley and come on back home. Come on! We'll scoot over there and do a little sabotage."

Johnny was silent. Fergie's plan bothered him—it was too much like high-school vandalism, slashing tires and stuff like that. On the other hand, he knew that they had to do something to stop the professor from going on his disastrous mission. At last he heaved a deep sigh and pushed his chair back. "Oh, okay!" he said as he shoved himself out of his chair. "Let's go over there and see what we can do. But remember that my key won't fit his front door lock anymore. And I'll bet you the front door and the back door are both fastened up tighter than a drum."

"I'll bet they are," said Fergie with a knowing smile. "But I wasn't gonna try to get in through the doors. There's four or five cellar windows over there, an' probably one of 'em is loose. Let's go see."

Johnny frowned doubtfully, but he followed Fergie out into the front hall. From the dining room came the sound of the baseball game that Grampa was listening to. Gramma was upstairs. Closing the front door softly behind them, the boys trotted across the porch, down the steps, and across the street. Without hesitating they ran around to the rear of the professor's house and plunged into the wet bushes that grew close to the stone foundation. Kneeling down, Fergie began to push at one of the cobwebbed cellar windows. It was stuck tight, and immediately Johnny's heart sank. But Fergie did not give in easily. He moved along to the second window and gave it a hard bang with the heel of his hand. With a squeak and a rattle it swung inward.

"See?" Fergie whispered. "What'd I tell you? Now get down on your hands and knees and follow me."

Johnny wanted to complain about the muddy ground that would get his pants all dirty, but he knew that Fergie would make fun of him, so he said nothing. He watched as his friend turned over onto his belly and slid feet first in through the narrow opening. Johnny hesitated—he really didn't like what they were doing.

"Come on!" Fergie called in a loud whisper. "What're you waitin' for? Christmas?"

With a deep sigh Johnny took off his glasses and put them into the holder in his shirt pocket. Carefully he lowered himself over the worn sill of the cellar window. It was pitch black down below, and when his feet hit, Johnny felt loose objects rolling around under him. Then he remembered—this was the window that led to the coal bin.

"Lots of nice dirty coal," said Fergie with a giggle. "Your gramma will love the way you look when you get back home."

Johnny winced, but he followed Fergie out of the coal bin and past the looming shadow of the furnace. Gradually their eyes got used to the darkness, and they moved across the cellar floor toward the tunnel. They could see a pale gleam coming from the archway. They knew that something was up.

"*Wait!*" Fergie whispered, and he put his hand on Johnny's chest. "We have to go really slow from here on."

Tiptoeing softly the boys made their way toward the glimmering brick passageway. They plastered their bodies against the rough wall and inched slowly along, sideways. The light at the far end grew brighter, and they could see the little red-and-green trolley car sitting on its rusty tracks. The shadow of a head bobbed behind the dusty windows, and in an instant the boys knew that their worst fears were true. The professor was getting ready to take the trolley on a trip back through time.

As they stood motionless, watching, an electrical hum filled the tunnel. The car shimmered like something seen through a rain-spattered window. There wasn't time to decide what to do. Both boys bolted forward and ran toward the little gilded balcony on the rear of the car.

The humming rose to an ear-splitting screech as the boys clattered up the metal steps and threw themselves, face-down, on the ridged steel platform. A howling wind sprang up, and the car shook violently. The trolley lurched forward, and Johnny clutched frantically at the floor, trying to get a handhold. A babble of confused voices filled his ears, and he felt as if his body was turning to sand, falling to pieces. *Oh, no . . . oh, no . . . oh, no . . .* he kept saying, over and over, and he hoped that he would lose consciousness. But he didn't, and the roaring, jolting ride went on.

CHAPTER SIX

The trolley finally stopped. Johnny felt scared and sick to his stomach, and his body was bruised because he had been thrown around during the ride. He had slammed against the trolley's rear door, and he had rolled over Fergie, who clung for dear life to the railing on the steel platform. As the two boys slowly picked themselves up, they felt a clammy, clinging chill, and they looked out at a drifting white mist that hung about the car. Where were they? In outer space somewhere? Or . . .

The rear door of the trolley opened, and the professor peered out. His face was deathly pale, and he was obviously much too frightened to be angry. The boys stared in wonder at him because he was wearing a long brown robe with a hood and, tied around his waist, a white braided rope. He wasn't wearing his glasses. After staring blearily at the boys for a few seconds, he reached inside the robe, pulled out his glasses, and put them on.

"Good merciful heavens, I *thought* so!" he muttered as he put his hand over his face. "Are you two completely, utterly out of your *minds*? By all rights you should have been swept away into the X dimension or some such place. But I see that God takes care of idiots, and here you are!" He took his hand away from his face and glowered at the boys. "Why on earth did you come? Don't you know that it was a very dangerous thing to do?"

Johnny stared stubbornly back at the professor. "We didn't care," he said firmly. "Fergie and I thought you might run off and do something crazy, and . . . well, we just didn't want you to get hurt. Did we, Fergie?"

Fergie shook his head. Like Johnny he was not at all ashamed of what he had done. But he was scared.

The professor was genuinely touched. His eyes filled with tears, but then he pulled himself together, *harrumph*ed, and tried to look dignified. "Gentlemen," he said in a strained voice, "I . . . I don't quite know what to say. It was good of you to be concerned about me, but . . . well, you know what a reasonable, restrained person I am. I would never do anything that would endanger my life."

Sure you wouldn't! thought Fergie, but he said nothing. Johnny began to glance nervously at the eerie, swirling mist.

"Where are we?" he asked in an awestruck voice.

"Where?" said the professor with a faint smile. "Well, out here you are between times, in the void, and if you step off this platform into the mist you won't be seen again, I promise you. But the trolley is hovering next to Leander's Tower, and once again we are ready to enter the long-lost world of 1453. By the way, in case you were wondering why I had my glasses off, I was trying to see if I could get along without them—they didn't have eyeglasses in the fifteenth century. Of course, I could use contact lenses, but I'm deathly afraid that I'll fall asleep with them on and suffer eye damage. I'm just running on, as usual: Come inside, and we can go out the side door as we did the other time. We won't stay long—just a couple of minutes."

Fergie and Johnny followed the professor through the door into the lighted interior of the car. Immediately both of them stopped and stared at a large bundle that lay on the floor between the rows of seats. There was the rubber life raft, and stuck under the straps that bound it was the professor's Knights of Columbus sword. On top of the heap lay an old, scuffed, black leather valise.

The professor's face got red. "I . . . I'll bet you're wondering what all this paraphernalia is for, aren't you?" he asked nervously.

Fergie grinned. "No, prof, as a matter of fact, we

weren't wondering! We saw you buy that raft downtown and we figured you were gettin' ready to make your move soon. We were gonna try and stop you—that's why we jumped on the trolley. You can't fool us—we can read you like a book!"

The professor coughed and glanced hurriedly away. "Well?" he said brusquely. "What on earth did you expect me to do? Eh? I've been thinking about Constantinople night and day ever since I found this ridiculous Time Trolley, and I just couldn't give up if there's even a tiny chance that I could save those poor people in the church."

Johnny's eyes grew wide "But professor!" he said in a puzzled tone. "What were you gonna do? I mean, you couldn't fight off the Turkish army all by yourself."

The professor's face got redder. He folded his arms and stared at the floor. "If you must know," he said quietly, "I was going to pretend to be an Angel of Light. Remember the legend I told you about? The people of Constantinople believed that an angel would come down into the great Church of the Holy Wisdom and drive away the enemy, even if the city walls had been battered down and all hope seemed to be gone. I know I don't look much like an angel, but . . . well, let me show you."

The professor bent down and undid the snaps on the black valise. He reached in and pulled out an odd-looking pistol. It had a stubby, tube-shaped barrel with a wide mouth. Johnny had seen guns like this in the movies, and he knew instantly that it was a flare pistol. Soldiers used them to signal their friends when they were in trouble. They fired the flares into the air, and the flares burst with a white or colored light, like Fourth of July skyrockets.

"I have a box of white flares in the valise," said the professor as he turned the gun over in his hands. "Normally they're set to explode at a great height, but I have shortened the fuses on these, so they will explode inside the dome of the church where the people will be hiding. I got the height of the dome from an architecture book that I have in my library. There'll be a flash of light, and some people will get their hair singed, but it ought to frighten the dickens out of the Turks. *That* is what I plan to do. The big problem will be getting into the city and getting back in one piece." He paused and looked hopefully at the two boys. "Do you think it would work?" he asked.

Johnny's eyes filled with tears. He knew that the professor was trying to do something fine and noble, but he felt that the plan was utterly, totally crazy. "Professor!" he pleaded, grabbing the old man's arms, "*please* don't do this! The raft will sink, or something awful that you don't expect will happen, and you'll get killed!"

Fergie clenched his fists and glared at the professor, who glared right back at him. Fergie was ready to wrestle the old man to the floor if he had to, and for a moment it looked as if there would be a fight. Then the professor laughed and tossed the flare pistol back into the valise. With a helpless sigh he sat down on the raft and folded his arms. "I hate to admit it," he said sadly, "but you boys are probably right. My plan is one that depends on everything going absolutely right, and any plan like that is a bad one. I'd probably wind up being captured and impaled by the Turks."

"Impaled!" said Johnny. "What's that?"

The professor winced. "Oh, it's just a charming punishment that the Turks used in the old days. They drove a sharpened stake through your body and left you to die in the hot sun."

Johnny was silent. Fergie hummed a bit and wound his watch, and the professor twiddled the tassels on the cord around his waist. After a long pause he adjusted his glasses and coughed nervously. Then he stood up and rubbed his hands impatiently. "*Well!*" he said, glancing from one boy to the other. "As long as we're here, we ought to go out and have a look at Constantinople from the windows of Leander's Tower. I promise you, on my solemn word of honor, that I will not do anything but look."

Johnny hesitated, but when he glanced at Fergie, he saw that he was raring to go. Silently the two boys lined up behind the professor at the side door of the trolley. He pulled the emergency cord and the doors hissed open. Then he reached into the folds of his robe and pulled out a small leather bag that hung from his neck by a piece of rawhide. Reaching inside, the professor plucked out the brass pipe tamper, and he used it to part the invisible veil that hung outside the trolley doors. Quickly the three stepped through.

Night lay over Leander's Tower. A streak of moonlight hovered on the rough stone floor of the room where the three travelers stood, and beyond the narrow windows they could see dark rippling water. The professor strode to one of the tall openings and stuck his head out. There was no glass in the window, so he was able to lean far out and look around. For a moment he was silent, but then—quite suddenly—he let out a loud exclamation. As the boys watched in astonishment, he turned on his heel and marched back to the veiled doorway that led to the trolley. Using the tamper he plunged through and disappeared. A few minutes later he came charging back with his valise and sword. Throwing the sheathed sword down on the floor beside him, he unsnapped the top of the valise and took out a large old-fashioned set of binoculars.

"I'm really worried," muttered the professor as he twiddled the adjusting wheel of the binoculars and used them to peer out the window. "There's a lot of activity on that shore over there. I really can't see a great deal in the dark, but there are torches flaring over on the far shore, and I think there are ships moving back and forth in the water. Lots of ships. That should not be, if we are here on March 30. But if one of the gears in that time machine has slipped, then—"

The professor's speech was interrupted by loud sounds that came from below. Yells and loud commands in a foreign language, and the heavy tramp of feet. Over in one corner of the tower room was a spiral staircase leading down. Torchlight flickered on the steps, and before anyone could move, a huge bearded man came vaulting up into the room. The man's face was ugly and scarred, and one of his eyes stared blankly off in the wrong direction. He wore a turban and a steel breastplate, and in his right hand he carried a long, curved sword. Behind him on the steps stood a grim-looking soldier who wore a pointed bronze helmet and carried a smoking, sputtering torch. The man with the turban began yelling at the professor and the boys in a strange language. They could not understand what he said, but the general meaning seemed clear: They were in the hands of the enemy, and they were in deep deep trouble.

CHAPTER SEVEN

Johnny, Fergie, and the professor stood dead still. They stared in horror at the fierce bearded man who was yelling at them. Johnny felt his stomach turn over. He closed his eyes and tasted fear in his throat. He wanted to think that this was a hideous dream, but it wasn't. It was very real and very frightening.

At last the professor pulled himself together. He muttered a word under his breath, and suddenly Brewster appeared over his left shoulder. Johnny and Fergie looked immediately at the bearded man to see what his reaction would be. But apparently he couldn't see Brewster, because he just went on ranting.

"For God's sake, please translate for me!" muttered the professor out of the corner of his mouth. "We're probably doomed, but at least I'd like to know what this fool is saying."

Brewster disappeared, and suddenly the bearded man was speaking English. But what he said did not make much sense.

"Butter and eggs, and a pound of cheese!" said the man huffily.

The professor ground his teeth. "Would you care to try again, you overrated hunk of stone?" he said.

"I'm trying! I'm trying!" said Brewster, and then—quite suddenly—the bearded man was saying things that made sense.

"I will ask you once more, and once only!" he roared. "Who are you and what are you doing here?"

The professor drew himself up to his full height and frowned. "In my satchel are many secret things that ought not to be tampered with by the likes of you," he declared solemnly. "As for ourselves, we are visitors here, and we are under the protection of your master, the Sultan Mehmet. He has sent us here to . . . uh, to read the signs in the heavens and see if the planets and stars are favorable for his attack on Constantinople. He will be very angry if you interfere with this important work."

The bearded man was astonished by this, but then his eyes narrowed suspiciously. "I am Baltoghlu, the Admiral of the Sultan's fleet," he growled, "and I never heard that the Sultan had hired a Christian monk to be his astrologer."

The professor smiled blandly. "Nevertheless," he replied, "the Sultan has friends who are not of the Moslem faith. He values learning and intelligence, even in those whose religion is different from his." This was true, and the professor knew it, but he wondered if this explanation would make any sense to Baltoghlu, who really did not seem very bright.

Baltoghlu seemed confused. He chewed his lip and glanced toward Fergie and Johnny. "What you say may very well be true," he said uncertainly, "but then who are these two, and why are they dressed so strangely? And why are two of you wearing glass discs over your eyes?"

Suddenly Fergie and Johnny realized that their clothing must seem very strange to the bearded man. They were wearing ordinary cotton shirts and corduroy pants, but no one in 1453 dressed that way. As for eyeglasses, they hadn't been invented yet.

However, the professor still thought that he could lie his way out of trouble. "These boys are from America, a land that lies far to the west," he said smoothly. "What they are wearing is their native costume. The glass discs are magic charms to ward off the spells of the Evil One." He took off the binoculars that hung from a strap about his neck, and with a polite smile he held them out for Baltoghlu to take. "Here," he said hopefully. "This is a powerful and magical seeing device. Take it and peer at the stars through it, and you will have wonderful visions."

Angrily Baltoghlu flung the binoculars into a far corner of the room. "I have no need of your magic rubbish!" he snarled. "And I don't believe anything that you have said. You three are my prisoners now, and you will come with me to see the Sultan. He will know whether you are lying or not!"

Baltoghlu barked a command, and two soldiers in chain mail stomped up the stairs. One soldier grabbed the valise and the sword and carried them away. The other one tied the hands of the three prisoners and hustled them down the narrow staircase till they came out into the open at a stone landing dock. There, bobbing on the waves, lay a long, narrow wooden ship. Two rows of oars sprouted from each side, and four stubby bronze cannon stood on the deck. A single mast rose from the middle of the ship, and a sail was tightly furled around one long yardarm. On the prow of the ship was a wicked-looking bronze beak that could be used for ramming other ships. This was a war galley—Johnny and Fergie had seen pictures of them in old books. And they knew that the oars were pulled by slaves who were chained in place, slaves who had to row endlessly until they died of exhaustion and were thrown overboard. Johnny shuddered. Would the Sultan condemn them to a punishment like that?

The three prisoners were shoved rudely onto the galley, and they were forced to sit down on the deck near one of the cannon. Anchors were hauled up, and the large, triangular sail was spread. The rhythmic hammering of a drum began, and the long oars began to move in rhythm. For a while the prisoners sat in silence. They watched the sailors as they moved to and fro on the deck, and they felt the ship surging along under them. Johnny felt sick, and he kept glancing at the professor, but it was so dark that he could not see the expression on the old man's face. Presently Johnny heard a twanging sound, and he turned to find Brewster sitting on the rail above their heads.

"So it's *you*!" muttered the professor sourly. "About time too! Is there anything you can do to get us out of this jam?"

"You really want a lot, don't you, whiskers?" said Brewster sarcastically. "I'm only a god of Upper and Lower Egypt, and my powers are somewhat limited. So I'm afraid you're going to have to take your chances with the Sultan. By the way, I hear that he's a thoroughly heartless man who would pull out his own grandmother's teeth if he—"

"I know all about the Sultan," snapped the professor irritably, "and I'll thank you to keep quiet about him for the time being. But look, isn't there *anything* you can do? I'm not asking you to turn pink and stand on your head. But can't you do something . . . well, scary and grand and super-colossal? Something that would frighten these wretches out of their underwear?"

Brewster was silent a moment. "There is something

that I *could* do," he said slowly, "but I'm allowed to do it only once every thousand years. And if it doesn't work, believe me, you'll be on your own. Do you want me to do it now?"

The professor thought a bit. They were in a jam, but they were not in the worst jam that he could imagine. Maybe he could sweet-talk the Sultan into letting them go. If the three of them were about to have their heads chopped off, then that would be a time for drastic action by Brewster. In the meantime it might be better to keep his powers in reserve. "No," said the professor at last, "I guess I don't want you to do your big fancy routine just now. I'll try to outwit the Sultan when we are brought before him."

"Good thinking," said Brewster. "By the way, I can offer you a small bit of cheery news. There is a ship headed this way, and it may belong to someone who is an enemy of the Turks. Then again it may belong to someone else—you never can tell."

The professor jumped. "A *ship*? God's teeth, man, are you *serious*?" Frantically he tugged at the ropes that bound his wrists.

"I was never more serious in my life," said Brewster calmly. "My eyes are quite good for seeing in the dark, and there is definitely a galley coming this way."

The professor's mind was racing. "If this is the middle of April—and it may very well be—then there are Venetian ships in these waters," he exclaimed hopefully. "The Republic of Venice sent ships to help the city of Constantinople, and some of them arrived and waited for the seige at the end of May. Lord in heaven, I hope I'm right!"

Johnny's heart leaped. He read a lot, and he knew that the city of Venice in Italy had once been a country all by itself. It had also been the center of an empire, controlled by Venice's powerful fleet. The Venetians were just about the best sailors in the world, and they were always fighting with the Turks to see who would control the Mediterranean Sea. If the ship that was coming toward them was from Venice, maybe they would be rescued.

Fergie had been silent for a long time, but he was not sitting around doing nothing. He was struggling with his bound hands to see if he could fish his switchblade knife out of his hip pocket. Unfortunately the pocket was buttoned, and that made things a little harder. After several unsuccessful tries he finally managed to unbutton the pocket and catch the handle of the knife between two fingers of his left hand. Slowly, carefully, he drew the knife out, and then he found the button and snapped the blade open.

"Scootch over here, John baby," he whispered, "and I'll see if I can cut your hands loose."

Johnny struggled around and held his hands out behind him, and soon he felt Fergie's knife sawing at the rope on his wrists. It seemed to take forever, and Johnny kept worrying that the Turks would notice what was going on. However, there was not much chance of that. They were running back and forth, getting ready for battle. Trumpets brayed and drums rattled, and loud, defiant shouts rang out. Meanwhile Fergie sawed away, and finally the last strand of rope parted and Johnny's hands were free. But just as that happened, a muffled roar was heard in the distance, and a ghostly plume of spray rose from the water near the Turkish ship's bow.

"Hey, they *are* on our side!" Fergie crowed. He held the knife out behind him, and soon Johnny was using the switchblade to cut loose his friend and then the professor. At last the three of them were free. Rubbing his sore hands, the professor jumped up. But he saw the soldiers running to and fro on the deck, and he quickly dropped back down to his knees.

"We've got to lie low for a bit," he whispered hoarsely. "When the battle starts, we'll make a run for it and see if we can get to my valise."

Johnny and Fergie crouched down under the shadow of the ship's rail as they heard a cannonball whiz past and crash into the galley's tall mast. With a loud creaking and groaning the mast fell, and the useless sail lay flapping wildly on the deck. A second later a loud crash split the air, as the ram on the enemy galley's prow smashed into the side of the Turkish ship. There was a long grinding and crunching sound, as oars broke and large splinters of wood flew in all directions. Johnny and his friends ran toward the shattered stump of the mast, and the professor got his hands on the valise. Quickly he tossed his sword to Johnny.

"Here! Defend yourself!" he yelled, but Johnny just clutched the sheathed sword in terror as men from the other ship poured over the rail onto the deck of the Turkish galley. All around him swords flashed, as the sailors and soldiers from the two ships fought desperately. Suddenly Johnny felt a sharp pain in his right arm. He looked down and saw that his sleeve was bloody, and when he looked up again, he saw a grinning, barechested sailor who was just in the act of raising his sword again to split Johnny in two. But at that second an arrow from a crossbow struck the man's neck, and he crumpled to the deck, dead.

The professor was struggling to load a flare into the flare gun. At last he was ready. He raised the gun and fired, and with a skyrockety *whoosh* the flare rose. It burst over the ship with a blinding white glare, and the soldiers on both sides threw themselves down on the deck and covered their eyes with their hands. With a triumphant yell the professor leaped onto the mast's stump and shouted, "*Surrender in the name of Venice!*" He didn't really know that the other ship was Venetian. He was just guessing. But sure enough, when the smoke from the flare's explosion had cleared, Johnny saw a soldier standing on the deck with a torch in one hand and a flag in the other. The flag was purple, and on it was embroidered the picture of a golden lion with wings, who was holding in his upraised front paw the tablets on which the Ten Commandments were written. The lion was the symbol of Saint Mark, the saint who watched over Venice. The Venetians had arrived, and the three travelers were saved . . . at least they hoped that they were.

CHAPTER EIGHT

Pale and shaken, Johnny clutched his injured arm. Near him Fergie and the professor stood dead still and waited to see what would happen. The Venetian galley's ram had smashed into the Turkish ship at an angle, and the two ships drifted on the water, locked together, while the acrid smoke of the flare still hung over them like a mantle of fog. The soldier with the purple banner hopped nimbly onto the deck of the Turkish ship and strode forward purposefully. He wore a shiny metal helmet that looked like an upside-down salad bowl, and his breastplate had an odd sort of metal skirt on the bottom. Behind him walked a short man with a well-trimmed beard. His face was sunburned and leathery, and his eyes were set in deep dark hollows. He wore a long red cape and a puffy velvet hat that looked like an oversized beret, and his battle armor was gilded and covered with fancy engraved decorations. In his hand he carried a glittering sword. The bearded man looked grim, and he stopped in front of the professor, looking him over from head to toe. For a long time he stared at the flare gun the professor held in his right hand. Then—to everyone's surprise—he smiled slyly, as if he had a secret.

The professor was very relieved. He bowed and began to speak, while Brewster hovered overhead and translated.

"Greetings, my lord!" the professor said. "I am a monk of the Franciscan order, and these are my companions. This weapon that I hold was invented by clever men in a far-off land. It frightens, but it's harmless."

The bearded man looked around at the Turkish soldiers and sailors who were still cowering on the deck with their hands over their eyes. "I see," he said. With a grand flourish he sheathed his sword and folded his arms. "You are under the protection of the Republic of Venice," he went on. "We have come to help the people of Constantinople, who are besieged, as you probably know. I am Admiral Piero Mocenigo, and I will aid you if I can."

"It seems like everybody's an admiral around this place," Fergie muttered to Johnny.

In a flash the man turned to stare at him. Again he

smiled as if he knew a joke that he wouldn't tell to anyone. "I beg your pardon," he said, "but I don't think I heard what you said."

Fergie's face turned red. "It wasn't important," he mumbled.

The Admiral laughed and turned quickly to the soldier who held the flag. He gave a quick series of orders: The Turkish prisoners were to be bound and the galley slaves were to be set free. A surgeon would be brought to bind up Johnny's wound, and after that was done, the old man and the two boys were to be treated with every courtesy. Soon they would have dinner with the Admiral in his cabin.

With a stiff bow the soldier turned away. When he was gone, the Admiral heaved a relaxed sigh and fixed the professor with a penetrating stare. "Your Italian is pretty good," he said in perfect English. "But I suppose that's the result of a first-class education. Where did you go? Harvard? Yale? Princeton?"

The professor's jaw dropped. How could this man know about American colleges that didn't exist in 1453? And where had he learned to speak with an American accent? When Brewster translated, everyone sounded British. What on earth was going on?

The Admiral broke up. He threw back his head and laughed. The professor was annoyed—if there was something funny going on, he wanted to know about it instead of being kept in the dark.

"Now see here!" he said crabbily. "You certainly aren't

an Italian admiral, and if you don't mind I'd like to know who . . ." The professor's voice died, and a light dawned in his eyes. "Good Lord, don't *tell* me!" he exclaimed. "You must be . . ."

The Admiral grinned. Without a word he held out his hand and showed the three travelers the large gold signet ring that he wore. On it were engraved the letters A.T.

Johnny blinked and stared at the man. "I don't get it," he said. "Who are you supposed to be?"

"Yeah," put in Fergie.

The professor gave the boys an exasperated look. "You two get F for Cleverness this week," he growled. "This is Aurelian Townsend, the man who built the Time Trolley that we used to get here. Remember? I told you that he disappeared mysteriously years and years ago. Well, here he is."

Johnny and Fergie were totally flabbergasted. They opened their mouths and closed them, but no sound came out. Finally Fergie spoke.

"Are . . . are you on the level?" he asked.

Mr. Townsend smiled blandly and nodded. "Indeed I am. It's very nice to meet you all. Wonderful, actually. I was beginning to think that no one would ever come back with the Time Trolley. You see—"

"Hey, wait a minute!" said Fergie suddenly. "How come you left the trolley and decided to come here?"

Mr. Townsend sighed. "I didn't have much choice in the matter, young man. The idling mechanism on the trolley went haywire, so the stupid piece of tin went zooming back to the twentieth century without me. I've been living in a monastery on the seacoast near here for the last several days, and I had begun to wonder if I was going to spend the rest of my life there." He paused, coughed, and glanced around nervously. "But see here," he went on hurriedly, "we can discuss this all later. These men here think I'm their admiral, so I guess I'll have to start acting like one." He turned away, cupped his hands to his mouth, and shouted several rapid-fire orders in Italian. Then he turned back to the three travelers and spoke to them in a low voice. "Come to my cabin with me. My surgeon is there, preparing a dressing for this young man's cut, and food is being brought. We can discuss what we ought to do next. Okay?"

The professor and the boys nodded, and they followed Mr. Townsend across a plank that had been thrown down to bridge the gap between the two ships. A little while later all four of them were sitting in a luxuriously furnished cabin in the Venetian galley. A surgeon washed the cut on Johnny's arm and bound up the wound with clean white cloth. Then he bowed and left, and everyone's attention turned to food. A large round table stood in the center of the room, and on it lay a bronze bowl full of figs, a jug of wine, and a loaf of bread. A tapestry hung on the rear wall of the cabin, and a carved wooden chest stood in one corner. From outside came a muffled clinking and hammering, and the raspy sound of a saw. Mr. Townsend explained that his men were freeing the galley slaves on the Turkish ship and repairing the hole that the Venetian ship's ram had made when it hit the Turkish galley. When the repairs were finished, Baltoghlu and his men would be forced to row the captured ship to a nearby island that was held by the Venetians.

"How did you ever wind up posing as a Venetian admiral?" asked the professor as he sipped wine from a bronze cup.

Mr. Townsend smiled smugly. "That," he said quietly, "was the result of an amazing piece of good luck. You see, when I came here, I was dressed as a monk, like you. So, after the Time Trolley had gone, I flagged down a fishing boat, and the men took me to a monastery near Rhegium, which is not far from here. Then, just the other day, this galley stopped in the harbor of Rhegium, and its commander was brought to our monastery on a stretcher. He had been badly wounded in battle, and it was clear that he was dying. While our monks were trying to save his live, I had a wonderful idea. The admiral was about my size, so I took his clothes and official documents, and I went to the ship and pretended to be a replacement for their leader. I made up some silly story about how I had ridden overland from Constantinople. I'm not sure if the men believed me, but they were glad to be at sea again. Then—"

"Wait just a minute," said the professor, jabbing a finger at Townsend. "Why did you want to leave the monastery? Did you decide that it would be better to die in battle than to die of boredom in Rhegium?"

Mr. Townsend laughed and shook his head. "Good gracious, no!" he exclaimed. "I had to get on this ship because I knew that the Time Trolley was coming."

Mr. Townsend undid the drawstring of a leather bag that hung on his belt. Plunging his hand into the bag, he pulled out a brass pipe tamper. It looked just like the one that the professor used to pierce the veil and let them into Leander's Tower. But there was one difference. This brass tamper was vibrating, and it kept changing color, from red to orange to green to violet and back again to red.

"This tamper is a bit fancier than the one you have," Mr. Townsend explained as he turned it back and forth between his finger and thumb. "It has a built-in alarm system that is supposed to warn me when the Time Trolley is near. I made it so that I could find my way back to the trolley if I got lost and couldn't remember where I had left it. Well, every day since the day I was stranded I have taken the tamper out of its bag, and I have prayed that someone would bring the bucket of bolts back to Leander's Tower. And now you folks are here. Once we have gotten rid of the Turkish galley, we will sail to Leander's Tower and take the trolley home—if it's still there."

Johnny felt suddenly queasy, and he glanced nervously at the professor. What on earth would they do if the trolley had gone without them?

The professor was confident. He brushed a speck of dirt off his robe and took a drink of wine. "I really wouldn't worry, Mr. Townsend," he said calmly as he set his goblet down on the table. "What happened to you was probably an exception . . . perhaps you didn't handle the controls of the trolley properly. I have made half a dozen trips in your machine, and it has always performed well for me. Of course, on this last trip it missed the date that I set it for, but I'm sure that the problem could be corrected if I fooled around with a screwdriver."

Mr. Townsend glared at the professor. He had built the Time Trolley, and he did not like to have this cranky little man telling him that he knew more about the machine than the inventor. But he restrained his anger, shoved his chair back, and stood up. "I have to go out on deck," he said, bowing stiffly.

He swept his red cloak about him, straightened the beret on his head, and marched out the door of the cabin. When the door had closed behind him, Johnny glanced quickly at Fergie, and he heaved a little sigh of relief. He was glad that the professor and Mr. Townsend had not argued, because he did not want anything to interfere with their trip home. There was a dull pain in his arm, and he wanted Gramma or Doc Schermerhorn to look at his cut and see if it was going to be all right. The sooner they were back in Leander's Tower, the better.

Minutes passed. Johnny, Fergie, and the professor munched figs while Mr. Townsend shouted orders on the deck of the galley. After half an hour had passed, the professor got fidgety. He hummed tunelessly and drummed his fingers on the table, and every now and then he said something under his breath. Finally Mr. Townsend came back to the cabin. He looked pale, and his mouth was set in a grim frown.

"It seems that we have a few problems," he said as he sank wearily into his chair. "When our ship rammed the Turkish galley, about half of the oars on our starboard side were sheared off. I'm afraid we're going to have to make the trip to Leander's Tower by just using our sail. Normally that wouldn't be too difficult, but there's a storm coming up."

The professor turned pale, and he swallowed hard. "A storm?" he said in a trembling voice. "Is . . . er, I mean, will it be a bad one?"

Mr. Townsend shrugged. "Who knows? Storms blow up very quickly in the Sea of Marmara, and sometimes they're pretty fierce. But we have to try to get to the tower. We're leaving right now."

The professor and the two boys followed Mr. Townsend out onto the deck of the galley. Overhead the great triangular sail moaned and strained against the wind, and the ship surged, cutting through the choppy water. But dark clouds had rushed in to hide the stars, and lightning flashed on the horizon. The ship began to pitch and roll, and the boys had to cling to the rigging to keep from falling down. Then, without warning, the wind changed direction. It blew straight against the sail, which flapped uselessly as the ship slowed down and then stopped altogether. But Mr. Townsend was not dismayed. He clung to a rope and bellowed loudly, "*Stand by to go about!*" The rudder swerved, and the ship's prow swung around in the opposite direction, running before the wind. The gale got stronger, and the sailors furled the sail up halfway, so that the force of the wind would not break off the mast. The ship heaved and tossed in the high, foamy waves. Now and then water broke over the railings and drenched the three travelers. Johnny felt cold and wet and very scared—would they ever get back to the tower? They were sailing the wrong way, but they really didn't have much choice. The night got blacker, and sheets of rain came slanting down. The loud howling of the wind drowned out all other sounds, and Johnny could not even hear himself praying. But his lips moved, and he kept saying the Our Father over and over. Suddenly the ship came to a grating, shuddering halt, and with a loud crack the mast snapped. The sail went over the side of the ship and lay fluttering on the water. In the distance, beyond the bow, Johnny saw the vague shapes of trees and a shadowy building. They had run aground on some unknown shore, and the ship was being pounded to pieces by the wind and waves.

Wildly Johnny looked around. Nearby he saw Fergie pulling himself to his feet. He had been knocked flat by the sudden stop, but he seemed to be all right.

"Come on!" Fergie yelled, grabbing Johnny by the arm. "We've got to get off of this crummy ship! Let's go!"

Johnny stared at the black choppy water and the pounding surf, and he was afraid. He could dog paddle around in a calm, heated pool, but he didn't know if he could swim in cold, churning sea. Fergie read his thoughts and dragged him over to the rail.

"It's okay!" he said soothingly as he pointed down. "The water isn't over your head. You can wade to shore. Come on!"

Johnny still hung back. All around them feet pounded on the galley's deck, and they heard loud splashes. Nimbly Fergie vaulted over the rail and landed in the water. Johnny looked down fearfully, and he was relieved to see that Fergie's head and shoulders were above the water.

"See?" Fergie yelled encouragingly. "It's not very deep! Come on! Jump!"

Johnny felt cold waves of fear sweeping over him; but he pulled himself together and clambered awkwardly over the railing. A second later his feet touched bottom. The two of them slogged through the water, which got shallower with every step. Suddenly a thought occurred to Johnny.

"Hey, Fergie!" he said anxiously. "Where's the professor?"

Fergie laughed. "He's up on the beach, waitin' for us! Right up there! See for yourself!"

Johnny looked where Fergie was pointing, and he saw the short elderly man squatting on a rock about halfway up the beach. He was clutching his valise to his chest, and the Knights of Columbus sword was stuck in the sand nearby. Johnny felt very relieved, and he waded faster. He stumbled up the beach and waved frantically at the professor, who was delighted to see him.

"Greetings, John!" said the old man, grinning toothily. "I see that you and Byron have survived the shipwreck. Have you seen Mr. Townsend?"

Johnny peered up and down the beach. It was a dark night, and it was very hard to see anything or anybody. "I don't see him anywhere," he muttered glumly. "Do you think he got drowned?"

The professor shook his head vigorously. "No, I don't think so," he said, smiling confidently. "If he survived for several days in this dangerous part of the world, he can certainly make it through a storm and a shipwreck. But see here! We're standing around babbling when we ought to be up and doing! Let's go find someplace where we can dry out and decide what to do next." He twisted around on the rock and looked toward the shadowy building that the boys had seen before. "Let's see what that place is like," he said as he got up. "It's very wet out here, and we're liable to catch cold if we don't watch out."

Fergie and Johnny followed the professor up the gravelly beach. Through the murk they could see a small stone building with a domed roof. Tall cypress trees waved in the wind nearby and cast weird shadows as the three travelers made their way to the arched doorway at the front of the building. The stout wooden door had been wrenched off its hinges and lay flat on the ground. Reaching into his valise, the professor pulled out his Nimrod pipe lighter. It was a tube about two inches long, and when he jerked at the ends, a spear of yellow flame shot out of the middle. With the lighter in his hand, the professor poked around on the ground till he found a piece of wood that he could use as a torch. It took several tries before he could get the wood to catch, but finally it burst into flame. Cautiously the professor moved through the gaping black archway and into the interior of the dark, abandoned building. What sort of house was this? The professor peered up at the domed ceiling, and he saw glittering gold mosaics. The staring faces of saints and angels looked down at them, and at once he knew where they were.

"This is a church!" he said in a hushed voice. "But look—the soldiers of the Sultan must have been here and looted it."

By the torch's wavering light the boys saw a stone altar at the far end of the building. It had been broken in two, as if someone had hit it with a huge sledgehammer. Strange symbols had been scrawled on the walls in red paint, and a broken sword and a couple of splintered spears lay on the dusty floor.

"Rotten vandals!" muttered the professor fiercely, and he kicked a piece of stone across the floor. "Can't leave anything alone, can they?" Glumly he pulled a bronze candlestick upright and stuck the torch in it. Then he tossed his sword and valise into a corner and sat down cross-legged on the floor.

Johnny slumped to the ground and sat there clutching his arm. It had begun to throb and ache fiercely now. "Professor?" he asked in a tearful, quavery voice. "What . . . what the heck are we gonna do? How're we gonna get a boat to take us back to Leander's Tower? My arm hurts like anything. Do you think that doctor on the boat knew what he was doing?"

The professor bit his lip. "That doctor was like most doctors in the year 1453. They didn't know anything but a few potions and salves. As for how we are going to get home, God knows! If Townsend is really dead, we will just have to find some fisherman and get him to take us to the tower. But our chances of finding someone to help us tonight are just about nil, so we'd better stay here where it's dry. Try to get some sleep, if you can."

It was silent. Fergie sat grimly staring at the leaping shadows cast by the torch. He wondered if he could defend himself against a Turkish soldier if one suddenly came leaping through the dark doorway. The professor stirred restlessly and got up. He knew that the wooden torch would not last forever, so he started poking around behind the ruined altar to see if he could find some candles. Johnny was feeling stranger and stranger. He imagined that he saw faces in the torchlight, the faces of ancient warriors. Outside, the wind was hissing through the cypress trees, but the sound was like excited whispering. What were they saying? He could almost make it out. . . .

"Professor," said Johnny suddenly, "there's . . . there's somebody outside."

The professor had just stepped back into the circle of light cast by the torch. In one hand he held two broken beeswax candles. Johnny's words startled him, and immediately his nerves were on edge. "How . . . how do you know?" he asked as he glanced quickly toward the gaping black doorway.

Johnny shook his head dreamily. "I dunno. I . . . I just know they're there, that's all."

Silently the professor put the candles down. He walked over into a dark corner and picked up the Knights of Columbus sword. Drawing the blade from the sheath, he padded to the doorway and peered out. Rain still swept by in sheets, and beyond the bending trees he could see the waves whipped into a froth by the wind. Moving across the water toward the shore was a long, narrow ship. Two soldiers in chain mail stood in the bow, holding torches aloft, and the light of the torches cast a lurid glare on the water. On glided the ship, noiselessly. Fear clutched at the professor's heart. What sort of creatures were these?

CHAPTER NINE

The sword dropped from the professor's numb fingers and clattered on the stone floor of the church. He backed away toward the circle of torchlight and stood tensely waiting. After many minutes he heard the sound of a boat's keel grating on the gravelly beach. Torches flared among the trees, but there was no jingle of armor or tramp of iron-shod feet. Finally a man appeared in the doorway. He was tall and grim-looking and wore a shirt of chain mail that reached to his knees. Over his armor he wore a sleeveless shirt of coarse white cloth with a large red cross stitched on its front, and a long sword hung from a belt around his waist. Quickly the man stepped over the threshold, and behind him came another, and another, and another . . . twelve in all. The silent warriors formed a ring around the three travelers. The torches flared yellow and smoky, and the professor could smell the burning pitch that the sticks of wood had been dipped in. As he glanced from one soldier to another, the professor saw that their faces were worn and scarred and blurry—as if the men were statues that had endured the wind and weather of several hundred years.

After a brief pause one of the soldiers stepped forward. He was tall and dignified, and he had a well-trimmed gray beard. Around his neck hung a golden chain from which a jeweled cross dangled. Quickly the man glanced down, and then he turned to the professor.

"Your friend is very ill," he said in a deep, grave voice. "He will have to come with us. You may come too if you wish."

The professor looked down, and with a shock he realized that Johnny was lying stiff and still on the floor of the church. What had happened? Was the cut infected, or . . . ?

As if in answer to the professor's thoughts, the bearded man spoke again. "The sword that cut him was anointed with a poison. We may be able to help, but we must go away from here."

Again the professor was stunned. How did this man know that Johnny had been cut by a sword? But before he could say anything, two soldiers stepped forward and gently picked Johnny up. Carrying him between them, they moved out through the doorway of the church.

The leader motioned with his hand, and the professor and Fergie followed as if they were hypnotized. Out the door and down to the beach they went, to the place where the long ship stood waiting. As before, it was surrounded by a halo of gray moonlight, though the sky was overcast and rain still fell. The two soldiers who carried Johnny laid him on a bed of fir boughs in the stern of the ship. The professor and Fergie clambered aboard with the others. Then the men shoved at the prow, and the ship slid back out into the water. The furled sail was raised, and instantly a wind started to blow, and the ship began to glide through the dark water. One man held the tiller at the stern, while the others stood still as statues along the sides of the vessel. Fergie and the professor made their way to the prow. They squatted on the damp boards and watched the high, carved prow of the ship rise and fall with the waves. Finally the professor spoke in a hoarse whisper.

"This is all very strange, Byron," he said as he glanced furtively over his shoulder. "These men are dressed like soldiers who lived two hundred years before the time we are in. They look like crusaders. To be more specific, they look like Templars."

Fergie's eyes opened wide. He knew the Templars were an order of monks who were also knights and warriors. "Templars, huh?" he muttered. "Well, what are they doing here? And where are they taking us?"

The professor shrugged. He was afraid of these strange, silent men, but he had a feeling that they would not harm him or his friends. And if Johnny was as ill as he looked, they would need all the help they could get to make him better. I wonder if I brought any gauze bandages along, thought the professor. With a jolt he realized that he had left his valise and sword back in the church. He sighed helplessly. Things really were out of his hands now, and he and the others would just have to go along and see what happened.

The ship drove on through the dark night. The trip seemed to take forever, and the professor wound up reciting all that he could remember of the *Iliad* in classical Greek. Fergie was silent, but he kept glancing anxiously toward the back of the boat, where Johnny lay. At last the darkness lightened to gray, and a yellowish dawn grew in the eastern sky. Up ahead rose a tall, humped island. At first it was just a purplish shadow rising from the sea, but as they drew closer, Fergie and the professor found that they were staring up at a high hill covered with dark, gloomy cypress trees. Between the clumps of trees stood white stone buildings that looked like tombs and rose up the sides of the hill, their dark doorways staring down like the eyes of skulls. At the top of the hill stood a circular stone fortress with battlements and narrow loophole windows. The whole place looked very forbidding, and there was no sign of any living person anywhere. In silence the ship sailed partway around the island, and then it plunged into a deep, rocky crevice. The sail was furled, and the ship coasted into a small, still lagoon that was sheltered by towering walls of limestone. Sand grated under the ship's keel, and the leader of the knights motioned for everyone to get out. Two soldiers carried Johnny up a winding staircase that was cut into the rock, and the others followed in single file. Last came the professor and Fergie, who felt more than ever that they had wandered into some very strange dream from which they might never awake.

At the top of the stairs rose the walls of the fortress, and the line of silent soldiers marched into the building through an open doorway. Fergie and the professor found that they were in a cavernous high-ceilinged chamber with a large fireplace at one end. A bright fire fought against the chill of early morning, and—to their surprise—they saw that a bed had already been prepared for Johnny. With great care the soldiers placed Johnny on the bed and drew a fur coverlet over him. Then, as the soldiers stood by like an honor guard, the leader of the knights knelt by Johnny's side and placed his hand on his forehead. He began to pray, and the words rose and fell like an incantation. Awkwardly the professor and Fergie looked on. They felt out of place here, and they also felt very hungry, since they had not eaten since early the night before. But it did not seem right to ask for food while these men were trying to save Johnny's life, so they said nothing. A soldier approached and laid his hand on the professor's arm. The professor shuddered because the hand was as cold as ice.

"You may eat now," said the soldier, and he gestured

toward a table at the far end of the room. Like a pair of clumsy children, the professor and Fergie followed the man to the table and sat down. The food was very plain—just cheese and bread—but the two of them felt that it was the best meal they had had in a long while. For the first time in many hours they began to feel optimistic. Suddenly they felt incredibly drowsy, and it occurred to them that they had not had much sleep. They slumped forward with their heads on the rough wooden table.

Many hours later Fergie and the professor awoke. The reddish light of late afternoon streamed in through a high window and hovered on the rough stone walls. The soldiers were gone. At the far end of the room Johnny lay motionless on his bed by the fire. Alarmed, the professor shook himself awake and got up. Had all this kindness and hospitality been a trick to put them off their guard? Had the leader of the knights been working for Johnny's death instead of helping him? As he rushed to the bedside, the professor saw that Johnny lay very still, and his face was deathly pale. Then—to his very great relief—he heard Johnny groan in his sleep, and he saw his chest rise and fall.

"He's alive, isn't he?" said Fergie, who was right beside the professor.

The professor nodded and tears trickled down his cheeks. Inside his head he heard a voice that said *You can do no good here*, and then he looked up and saw the leader of the knights standing near him. The man's eyes were kindly, but his mouth was curled into an amused smile.

"Go out and enjoy the island," he said softly. "Evening is drawing on, and this place is beautiful at night. The night air will do you good."

The professor was awed and a bit frightened by this man, but he had to ask a question. "Is . . . is Johnny going to live?"

The knight looked grave. He stared for a long time at the pale form that lay on the bed. "Ask me in an hour's time," he said. "In the meantime please go outside. You are not helping him by kneeling here."

Reluctantly the professor and Fergie turned and walked out through the stone archway and down a short flight of cracked, weathered steps. The sun was setting, and shadows deepened under the cypress trees that grew everywhere on the island. A night wind began to blow. It stirred the trees and made an eerie whispering sound, and Fergie and the professor imagined that they heard voices talking of sorrows long past and bitter griefs that still stung the heart. They walked on and finally stopped outside one of the strange, white, tomblike buildings that they had seen from the ship. Up close the gaping black doorway seemed even more forbidding than it had seemed from a distance. Fergie and the professor hurried on past another white tomb and another and another. Finally, out of breath, they stopped at a place where the path looked out across the darkening sea.

"Prof?" Fergie asked anxiously. "What . . . what is this place, anyway?"

"It is the Isle of the Dead," said the professor grimly. He didn't know why he said this—the words just came floating into his brain. "As for those strange, silent knights," he went on, "they are ghosts. Long ago when they were alive, they were part of the Crusader army that in 1204 looted and burned Constantinople out of pure greed. Now they are being punished, it seems: Their spirits haunt this place."

Fergie was thoroughly frightened by now. "Are . . . are they gonna kill us?" he asked in a faltering voice.

The professor shook his head. "No. I'm pretty sure that they are trying to help us. Perhaps if they perform enough good acts, their spirits can rest. I certainly hope they can help us. By God, I *hope* so!" The professor swallowed hard, and he tried to choke down a sob. He was thinking of Johnny.

After a few minutes they turned and walked back up the path. They did not know if an hour had passed, but they did not want to wander about anymore on this weird island. Far above, at the top of the path, they saw the arch lit by flickering firelight. When they finally got to the entrance, they saw a strange scene. All the knights were standing in a circle around Johnny's bed, and the leader was kneeling by him with a small bronze bowl in his hand. He dipped his fingers in the bowl and smeared something—it looked like ointment—on Johnny's forehead. Again the sound of praying rose into the high roof of the chamber. Fergie and the professor stood in the doorway a long time, as if they were stone statues. They did not move as they watched the strange, solemn ritual go on. At last the chanting stopped, and the leader of the knights rose and walked to the doorway. Fergie and the professor could see that his face was sad. They braced themselves for the bad news that was probably coming.

"How . . . how is he?" asked the professor in a weak quavering voice.

The leader shook his head. "Not good. Not good at all. The poison is a strong one, and I cannot fight it much longer. If your friend is to live, a greater power than ours will be needed."

The professor stared. "For heaven's sake tell me what to do!" he exclaimed vehemently. "Johnny is my dearest friend in all the world, and I don't want him to die."

The leader gazed long and hard at the professor. "You must take him to Constantinople. Near the great Church of the Holy Wisdom is a smaller church that holds the most sacred picture in all Byzantium. It is called the Hodegitria, and its power is much greater than ours. You must press the young man's hand to the Madonna's face in the painting. If he lives till you get him there, the Hodegitria may save him."

The professor thought of the Turkish army that was gathering outside the great walled city. He thought of the Turkish ships that were patrolling the waters near the city's harbors. "How on earth am I going to get into the city?" he exclaimed in despair. "I'd need a Sherman tank, and I'm afraid I didn't bring one with me. Can *you* take us in through one of the gates?"

The leader shook his head gravely. "No. We did great wrong to the city many years ago, and we may not enter it. But we can bring you to the gates and help you to enter." The leader paused and gazed deep into the professor's eyes. "Believe me," he said solemnly, "I would not send you and your friends into danger if there was any other way. But there is not—you must go if your young friend is to live."

CHAPTER TEN

With the professor and Fergie following behind, the soldiers carried Johnny down the long winding stair that led to the sheltered harbor where the ship lay waiting. It was a calm, starry night without a breath of wind, but the professor knew that would be no problem for these strange, ghostly knights. As soon as everyone was on board, the leader raised his hand imperiously, and the large square sail began to fill. Slowly the ship sailed out through the narrow inlet and into the open sea. As before, Fergie and the professor sat in the stern and Johnny lay in the bow. Except for the man who gripped the tiller and steered the ship, the knights stood grouped around the mast, with their leader in the midst of them. The whole scene was like something out of a King Arthur story, and at another time the professor might have been moved by the beauty of it all. Instead he bit his lip impatiently and kept urging the ship on with silent cries of *Faster, blast you! Faster!* He did not know how long Johnny had to live, and he felt that every second counted. He began to think about Brewster—where on earth was he? He had not been heard from since Mr. Townsend's ship had gotten wrecked near the ruined church. Maybe he had been hovering invisibly and translating for them, but the professor doubted it. The knights probably didn't need help to talk to ordinary mortals. "Oh, well," the professor muttered, "he's probably out there somewhere!"

"I didn't catch that. What did you say?" asked Fergie, who was squatting right next to him on the damp deck of the ship.

"Nothing," said the professor crossly, and he went back to studying the stars.

After a while the professor got tired of sitting, so he hauled himself to his feet and picked his way over to the starboard side of the ship. Clinging to the rail he looked out, and he saw the shadows of walls looming under the starlit sky. The professor had studied maps of Constantinople for a long time, and he knew that the city was built on a piece of land that was roughly triangular in shape. Two sides of the triangle faced the water, and the walls came right down to the sea. The current was swift here, and there was no way that the enemy could land troops outside the sea walls or plant ladders there. The vast army of the Sultan had gathered outside the land walls; they were out there in the darkness somewhere, getting ready to attack the city with all their strength and savagery. Of course—the professor thought gloomily—the Turks may have been here for quite a while. The Time Trolley had screwed up the date of their arrival, and God only knew what day it was. And it wouldn't do any good to ask someone, because the people of 1453 used a calendar that was different from the one in use in the twentieth century. Phooey! thought the professor. Phooey on everything, anyway!

The ship surged on, and the professor heard a dull *boom!* in the distance. The Turks must be firing their great cannon, the one that they would use to batter down the thousand-year-old walls of the city. The shadowy walls loomed closer. In his mind the professor tried to reconstruct the way Constantinople was laid out. If we are trying to reach the church where the painting of the Hodegitria is, we will have to head for . . . hmm, let me see . . . for the Gate of the Lighthouse. Yes, that's definitely the one. And sure enough, as he clung to the rail and strained his eyes, the professor saw a wavering blot of orange light in the distance. That would be the light of the Lighthouse, which of course was just a tall stone tower with an iron basket of fire on top. Wood and pitch fed the flames in the basket—this was the best people could do in the days before electricity was invented. The light got closer and closer, and the professor saw a stone breakwater rising from the sea. Behind it was a small harbor, and near the tower that held the flaming light, a wide arch gaped. But the arch was sealed by a stout, iron-bound door, and no doubt there were heavy bars in place on the inside. This was a time of war, and no one, absolutely no one, friend or foe, would be admitted.

Silently the ship glided into the little harbor. It pulled up to the stone breakwater and hovered there, as if held by invisible ropes. The leader of the knights left his place by the mast and walked back to join Fergie and the professor. A halo of gray light hovered about his gray, weatherbeaten face.

"You must leave now," he said quietly. "Follow me up onto the stones."

The professor blinked and stared unbelievingly. "God in heaven, man!" he exclaimed indignantly. "Are you just going to *leave* us here?"

The leader looked offended. "Did I not say that I would get you into the city?" he said. "Be patient, and all will be made clear."

The professor shrugged helplessly and followed the leader to the middle of the ship. There a ribbed wooden ramp had been erected to make it easier to get to the breakwater. Fergie and the professor watched as two knights carried a stretcher with Johnny's still form up the ramp. Then they joined the leader up on the slimy stones. Reaching in under the white surcoat that covered his suit of chain mail, the leader brought out an odd-looking brass object. It looked like this:

The professor and Fergie stared as the leader held the object up. It glimmered faintly in the starlight.

"This is a Tabergan," he said gravely. "It is good for taking people up into the air and putting them down where they want to be. Simply twist the handle and say, 'Go where I say, Tabergo, Tabergan!' Then tell it where you want to go and twist again. It is extremely reliable and will not fail you."

The professor looked doubtful, but he held out his hand as the leader offered him the brass Tabergan. It felt cold and rather heavy. The professor opened his mouth to thank the leader, but the man turned away abruptly and led his soldiers down the ramp into the ship. Suddenly the professor thought of something that he needed to ask.

"Will this work for only one person?" he called, "or will it take all three of us?"

The leader's voice came drifting up, hollow and disembodied. "If you cling to each other, it will take you all." And with that the ship began to glide away. Soon it was a glimmering smear of gray light on the dark sea.

The professor sighed and stared up at the grim city walls. Then he looked at the object in his hand. He did not feel very confident. In fact, he felt scared and alone, and had to keep fighting down the panic that rose inside him.

"It looks like the spigot on a beer barrel," said Fergie helpfully.

"Yes, doesn't it ever!" muttered the professor gloomily. "Come on, let's see if this doohickey works."

Fergie stooped and grabbed Johnny's limp hand. With his other hand he reached up and gripped the professor's arm. The professor took a deep breath and let it out. He seized the handle of the Tabergan and twisted it. "*Go where I say, Tabergo, Tabergan!*" he intoned, and then he added, "*Take us over the wall!*" Another twist, and the three of them were sailing up into the air and over the stone battlements. It was a sickening feeling, waving your feet at nothing while some force bore you upward, and it reminded the professor of the time he had ridden on a ski lift. They descended, and with a jolt and a bump the three travelers landed in the middle of a rough, cobblestoned street. The professor came down hard on his feet, and a sharp pain shot up to his knees.

"Heavens!" he growled. "Do people *always* get dumped this way?"

"At least we made it," said Fergie with a sour grimace. He looked down at the still figure that lay on the stones near them. "I hope it didn't hurt John too much to land like that."

Both of them knelt and examined their friend. His hair was limp and soaked with sweat, and he seemed to be barely breathing. Johnny's right sleeve had been cut away, and his arm had been bandaged where the sword had cut it. When he touched the arm gently with his fingers, the professor was shocked at how hot it felt. "Come on, Byron!" he said as he pulled himself to his feet. "Let's get to that church while we have time!"

With a muttered prayer of thanks, the professor tucked the Tabergan into a pocket of his robe. The stretcher had not come over the wall with them, so he had to put his hands under Johnny's armpits while Fergie grabbed his legs. Slowly, with a lot of grunting, they lugged their friend along, and the professor began to look around to see if he could get his bearings. They were in a narrow street lined with dark stone houses, and wavering shadows cast by the lighthouse shone on the walls. Racking his brain the professor struggled to remember the layout of this part of the city. The little church where the Hodegitria was kept ought to be up ahead somewhere, not far away. Sure enough, as he turned his head and craned his neck, he saw at the top of the gently rising road a small, whitewashed building with an arched roof. "That has to be it!" he muttered through his teeth, and he shuffled along faster with his load. The two of them slogged on, trying hard not to drop their unconscious friend, until they paused before the door of the church. From the distance came the sullen flat boom of the Sultan's cannon. How long would it be before the city was taken? No time to think about that now—they had to get into the church.

Gently Fergie and the professor laid Johnny down outside the worm-eaten wooden door. Stepping boldly forward the professor seized the twisted wrought-iron ring that hung from the door and shoved. With a strange half-human groan the door swung inward. Fergie and the professor saw the dimly lit interior of the church. Bronze lamps hung from the ceiling and cast a smoky light over the altar at the far end. Propped on the altar was a painting in an elaborately jeweled frame. It showed a mother and her child, and their heads were surrounded by gilded haloes. A smell of incense hung in the air, and before the altar one old woman knelt. Fervently she clasped her hands together as she prayed in words that neither Fergie nor the professor could understand.

For about half a minute the professor and Fergie stared awestruck at the scene. Then, carefully, they lifted Johnny's limp form and carried it through the doorway. They headed straight toward the altar, as the old woman gaped in amazement. The topazes and rubies and opals and carbuncles in the picture's frame twinkled and glimmered under the lamplight. The mother and child stared out eerily at the visitors, and the professor half expected them to speak. Sadly he thought of what would happen to the picture when the Turks took the city: It would be ripped from its frame and hacked into pieces. Fergie and the professor laid Johnny on the altar and raised his right hand till it touched the face of the staring woman. At that moment a wind blew in through the half-open door of the church. The lamps swayed and rattled, and weird leaping shadows flew over the whitewashed walls. The professor and Fergie watched Johnny's face intently. At first nothing happened, but then color flowed back into his pale cheeks, and his eyelids began to flutter. He groaned and looked up at his friends.

"Hey . . . wha . . . where are we?" he mumbled thickly. He remembered falling asleep in the ruined church by the seashore.

But this was a different place.

"Thank God!" said the professor as his eyes filled with tears. He heard Fergie sniffling beside him, and he knew that he too was incredibly relieved.

"You are in Constantinople, John," said the professor. "And you have just narrowly escaped death—"

The professor was cut off by a loud noise. The door of the church was flung violently open, and in rushed an elderly monk in a black robe. With him were half a dozen soldiers in gleaming breastplates and bronze helmets. They carried drawn swords and looked angry. The monk was furious, and he marched halfway to the altar before he stopped and began yelling in a strange language. The three travelers had no idea what the monk was saying, but the general meaning was clear. They were up to their necks in trouble again.

CHAPTER ELEVEN

The monk went on ranting, and the soldiers advanced threateningly toward the three travelers. The professor thought of Baltoghlu, the man who had captured them in Leander's Tower. "I've read this script before," he muttered to himself bitterly. Suddenly he found that he could understand the monk, and he knew that Brewster had returned, though he couldn't see him.

"Soldiers, do your duty!" the monk barked. "Arrest these three sorcerers. With my own eyes I saw them fly over the wall. They have come here to steal the holiest painting in all of Byzantium. No doubt they were sent here by the Sultan, to take away the sacred power of the Hodegitria and weaken our defenses. Arrest them, I say!"

The professor's heart sank. He knew that the defenders of Constantinople had only a few thousand men to defend fourteen miles of walls, so he really had not been surprised when no sentries challenged them from the walls above the Gate of the Lighthouse. But the monk had been there, hiding, and he had seen every move that they made after they landed. What rotten luck! thought the professor. He also thought about what they did with sorcerers and witches in the year 1453—they burned them at the stake.

There was no point in arguing. Meekly the professor and the boys let the soldiers tie their hands behind their backs, and then they were hustled out of the church. In the street outside the monk signaled for the soldiers to stop. He had noticed the bulge in the pocket of the professor's robe and wondered what it was. He boldly dipped his hand into the pocket and pulled out the Tabergan. Again the professor felt despair. Why hadn't he thought quickly enough and gotten the boys to cling to him while he used the Tabergan to whisk them away? But everything had happened so quickly that there had been no time for lightning-quick action and clever, resourceful ideas.

"What a fascinating object!" said the monk, grinning evilly. "Explain its purpose to me!"

"As long as I'm going to die, I see no reason why I should be helpful," growled the professor.

Cold hatred gleamed in the monk's eyes. A vein began to throb in the side of his long, skinny neck, and he thrust his face forward till he and the professor were practically nose to nose.

"If we were back in Spain, where I come from," the monk snarled, "I would find ways to make you cooperative! The rack does wonders to make people helpful. But alas, the Emperor does not approve of such methods." He paused and glanced off into the darkness. "Never fear, though," he went on wickedly, "I have some authority in this part of the city, and I can have you put in prison. Tomorrow morning you will be devoured by flames in a courtyard."

Fergie started to yell at the monk, but a soldier slapped his face and he fell silent. The Emperor's soldiers began to drag the three struggling captives away across the rough, cobblestoned street. But before they had gotten far, a dull *boom* sounded in the distance, and at almost the same moment a man in a purple tunic came dashing around a corner with a torch in his hand. Embroidered on his shirt front was a gold eagle, which meant that the man was a messenger from the Emperor. When he saw the soldiers with their odd-looking captives, he stared in disbelief.

"My good men, what are you doing?" he cried indignantly. "The enemy is at the gates! Do you not hear the sound of battle in the distance? We need every man who can carry a sword! Come with me to the western walls! At *once!*"

The soldiers paused and looked doubtfully at each other. "Now see here!" the monk roared. "What gives you the right—"

The messenger cut him off. "*This* gives me the right!" he snapped, pointing to the gold eagle on his shirt front. "Go to your church and pray, old man, pray hard that we will be rescued from the hands of our bloodthirsty enemies!" He beckoned to the soldiers. "You men come with me! That is an order from the Emperor Constantine!"

The soldiers let go of their captives and followed the torchbearing messenger down the street. They had not taken three steps when the professor called out loudly to Johnny and Fergie, "Run for it!"

Awkwardly, with their hands still bound behind them, they dashed away into the shadows, while the monk ranted at them, "Come back, you hounds of Satan! You must suffer punishment for your wickedness! *Come back!*"

But the professor and the boys were not listening. Blindly they dashed away down a pitch-dark alley and ran across a rough, uneven field till they came to a place where huge shadows loomed before them. Some vast stone structure towered above them, and they plunged in through a cleft that opened into an enormous oblong space. Tiers of stone seats rose up on all sides, and they could see the stars above them. Suddenly the professor knew where they were.

"This . . . this is the Hippodrome!" he gasped, leaning against a stone seat to catch his breath. "They used to have chariot races here, and the whole city turned out to watch. Maybe we can hide here until we figure out what to do next."

Nobody had any better ideas, so they settled down in the Hippodrome for the night. First, though, Fergie fished in his back pocket to get his switchblade and cut his friends free. When they were all untied, they huddled down under a big stone seat that had probably held some dignitary back in the days when the chariot races were popular. Every now and then they heard a cannon boom in the distance, but they were so far away from the city's western walls that they could not hear the din of battle.

"I wouldn't worry about it in any case," muttered the professor sleepily as he settled back against a stone wall. "The city was taken around four in the afternoon on May 30. Nobody's going to get in in the middle of the night."

"That's nice to know," said Fergie sarcastically. "So what happens if tomorrow is the thirtieth of May?"

The professor was silent. Fergie did have a point. The Trolley had really screwed up their date of arrival, and it was possible that they were here sometime in late May. That was a very discouraging thought. "Tomorrow morning," he said with determination, "we are going back to that church, and we are going to find that monk and swipe the Tabergan back from him. You know, if he had come into the church five minutes later, we would have been gone. As soon as you were cured, John, I was planning to whisk us all away to Leander's Tower. But the best-laid plans, et cetera, et cetera. Phooey!"

"If you don't mind my saying so," said Brewster out of the darkness, "that is a pretty dumb idea. That monk may be at the other end of the city by morning. Or he may have found some more soldiers, and you will be outnumbered in any fight that occurs."

"Thank you for your wise advice," growled the professor. "It's nice of you to reveal yourself to us at last. Where the devil have you been?"

"Around," said Brewster casually. "When those Templar ghosts arrived, I figured you were in good hands, so I left. Since then I've been wandering up and down the coast looking for that Townsend character. I found him wandering along the shore, not far from that ruined church you were holed up in. It's just outside the western wall of the city. He looked a bit vague, but I think he's okay, and he seems to be your only ticket out of this place. If you can get him to flag down a Venetian ship, maybe you can con the sailors into taking you back to Leander's Tower. Is that a good idea?"

"It has its points," said the professor dryly. "But would you mind telling me how we are going to get to the western side of the city with the Turkish army in the way?"

"I have an answer for everything," said Brewster smugly. "And if you people will put off snoozing for a little while, I can show you a secret tunnel that has not been used since the days of Constantine the Great, the founder of this city. Are you interested?"

Wearily the professor tried to wake up. If Brewster was right about the tunnel, it might be better to search for it than to wait for a chance to grab the Tabergan back.

"Where does this tunnel go?" asked the professor warily.

"Out to a dry well in a grove of trees that is just beyond the western walls of the city. That would put you not far from the last place where I saw Townsend. Neat, eh?"

The professor ground his teeth. "Oh, just peachy keen!" he said sarcastically. "And how, pray tell, do you know about this tunnel?"

"I know lots of things," said Brewster blandly. "I've been here before, a couple of times. When Justinian was emperor—boy, did they have the parties then!—I remember—"

"Oh, spare me, please!" sighed the professor as he dragged himself to his feet. "Come on, boys, we're going hunting."

With bewildered frowns on their faces, Fergie and Johnny followed the professor and Brewster. Brewster glowed with a pinkish light, and he bobbed along about two feet off the ground, humming tunelessly all the while. They padded down the weedy, unused racetrack till they came to a place where the track took a wide rounded turn. To mark the turn, a bronze pillar on a tall stone base had been erected. Brewster paused by the pillar's base and hovered there in the dark.

"This is where the tunnel starts," he said. "No one has used it in a long time, because you need a password to make the entrance open up, and the password has been forgotten."

"Do you know what it is, Brewster?" asked Johnny eagerly.

"No," said Brewster. "I'm afraid not."

"Well, isn't that just fine!" the professor growled. "How on earth are we going to get the blasted thing to open?"

"Don't get all hot behind the ears, whiskers," said Brewster soothingly. "I think the clue to the password is carved on the stone base of the pillar. Have a look."

Grumbling, the professor fished his Nimrod lighter out of an inner pocket of his robe and snapped it on. By the lighter's smoky glare, the boys saw part of a long Latin inscription, and below it some faintly carved symbols:

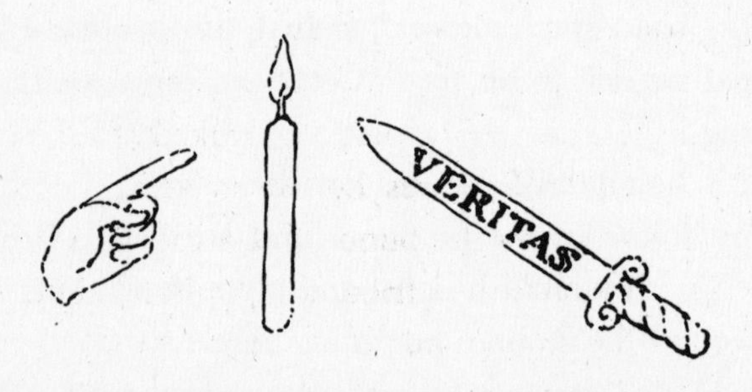

A pointing hand, a candle, and a sword inscribed with the Latin word for truth—what did all this mean?

"Hmm," muttered the professor as he scratched his chin. "This reminds me of something, but what? It probably refers to some familiar phrase—not familiar to twentieth-century people, but familiar back in ancient times. What could it be?"

For a long time the professor pondered, pacing back and forth in front of the pillar's base. Suddenly his thoughts were interrupted by a loud shouting noise and the glare of torches at the far end of the stadium.

"Oh, good merciful heavens!" exclaimed the professor, putting his hand over his face. "It must be that rotten monk, and I'll bet he's found some more soldiers! What filthy luck! Let me see . . . let me see . . . it must be something simple! A pointing hand . . . point to a light and to the sword of truth . . . wait, wait, I've almost—" The professor let out a loud roar of triumph: "I'VE GOT IT!" Pausing to pull himself together, he said loudly and clearly, "*Send forth thy light and thy truth, O Lord!*"

Nothing happened. Not far away, the monk and his soldiers could be seen by the bouncing glow of torches. Johnny and Fergie turned pale and looked at each other. They imagined themselves bound to stakes while the evil monk set fire to the bundles of sticks piled around them. The professor had tried, and he had failed. What was going to happen now?

But the professor did not give up so easily. As the enemy raced closer, he stood his ground and tried to think, forcing his mind to turn over like an old tired car engine. Suddenly he snapped his fingers. Closing up the lighter, he folded his arms and cried out, "*Emitte lucem tuam et veritatem tuam, Domine!*" Immediately a loud crunching and grinding sound began. The earth shook, and as the three watched, the great bronze pillar swung slowly to one side, revealing a square opening. Again the professor lit his Nimrod lighter, and they saw shadowy steps leading down. With the loud shouts of the angry monk ringing in their ears, the two boys and the professor went stumbling down the steps. At the bottom the professor paused, searching frantically for some way of closing the opening. As he held the lighter up and peered around, the professor saw an inscription in a rectangular border. It said CAVE CANEM, which means "Beware of the dog." This made no sense at all, but the professor was not in a sensible mood, so he just yelled, "*Cave Canem!*" Sure enough the pillar began to swing back into place. They got a glimpse of angry faces crowded around the rapidly shrinking opening, and then with a shuddering slam the hole was closed, and they were safe.

"My word!" sighed the professor as he mopped his forehead with his sleeve. "That was a close one. Needless to say, the Latin version of the phrase was what we needed." Hastily he glanced around at the boys, who were standing nearby in the darkness. "Are you two all right?" he asked.

"I guess so," said Johnny uncertainly.

"Yeah, we're okay," Fergie added bravely. "Let's get this show on the road. Lead on, prof!"

In single file they began to pick their way down the long, dark, echoing tunnel. Brewster's bobbing pink light led the way, casting a faint pinkish sheen on the ancient barrel-vaulted ceiling and the mossy stones underfoot. Now and then something would crunch under Johnny's foot, and he would look down and see that he had crushed the skeleton of a long-dead rat. In one place the stones of the ceiling had fallen, and they had to wade through greenish stagnant water and pick their way over muddy granite blocks. Finally, after what seemed like ages, they passed through a low arched doorway and found that they were standing at the bottom of a tall, circular stone shaft. This was the dry well that Brewster had spoken of earlier. They had reached the end of their underground journey. Stone steps wedged into the wall spiraled toward the sky, and they climbed slowly. Johnny was terrified. If he missed his footing, he would go hurtling down the well shaft, and that would be the end of him. But he knew that this was the only way out, and so he plodded doggedly on, with the professor in front of him and Fergie behind. Finally, one by one, they clambered up over the worn lip of the well and stumbled out into a dark, rustling forest. The professor wanted to search for Mr. Townsend, but he had not brought a compass with him, and there was no point in wandering around aimlessly in the dark. Besides, he was dead tired, and so were the others. After a quick look around the professor threw himself down on the grass near the well, and the boys lay down near him. In a very few seconds all three were asleep.

When dawn came, they awoke to the sound of birds twittering in the trees. Massive oaks crowded around them, but the early daylight came slanting in through the leafy boughs. The professor rose. Quickly he shook the boys and hauled them to their feet. They complained sleepily, but the professor had a vague idea that they were near the Turkish camp. If that was so, they had better get away toward the seashore while they could. When he shielded his eyes and peered toward the rising sun, he could see open country beyond the trees. After ordering the boys to follow him and be silent, he crept cautiously forward till he stood at the edge of the forest. Beyond lay grassy hills, which sloped off toward a little river valley on the left. A few hundred yards away stood the walls of Constantinople. Here, on the land side, it was a triple wall—first a low breastwork, then a twenty-foot-high wall with towers, and finally a forty-foot-high wall with still more towers. The walks on top of the walls were thronged with soldiers, and flags flew from many of the towers. Peering far off to the left, the professor saw that the ground was black with soldiers. It looked as if the Turkish army was getting ready for an attack. Turning back, the professor glanced toward the rolling grassland that lay between him and the city walls. He had seen something out of the corner of his eye. He looked again, and his mouth dropped open. A man was strolling casually along. He wore a puffy purple hat and a red cloak, and he was carrying the professor's black-leather satchel. A sword in a black, silver-mounted scabbard was slung over his shoulder. It was Mr. Townsend, and he was heading for the city walls. He acted as if he did not have a care in the whole wide world.

CHAPTER TWELVE

Fergie, Johnny, and the professor stared. They were utterly flabbergasted.

"Holy Mother Macree!" exclaimed the professor. "What on *earth* does that fool think he's doing? Come on! We've got to stop him before he gets himself killed!"

As Fergie and Johnny watched in horror, the professor bolted out of the clump of trees and began running toward Mr. Townsend. After glancing quickly at each other, the two boys began running too—there didn't seem to be anything else they could do. For an old man the professor could really scoot. Fergie caught up to him first, and he saw that the professor was holding Mr. Townsend by the arm and talking to him rapidly. The sword and the valise were lying on the ground nearby.

". . . and so we've got to get back to the trees," the professor was saying as Fergie drew near. "The whole Turkish army is out there, and pretty soon they'll see us, if they haven't done so already. Come on! We have to go back!"

Mr. Townsend glowered at the professor. He set his feet stubbornly and refused to move. "Take your hands off me!" he said haughtily as he tried to shake his arm free from the professor's grip. "I am an admiral of Venice. The Emperor of Byzantium needs me, and I am going to his aid! I found an enchanted sword and this bag of enchanted objects in a half-ruined church near here. With these weapons we will beat back the enemy. I order you to let me go! If you do not, the wrath of Venice will fall on your head!" Once again Mr. Townsend tried to wriggle free, but the professor's grip was like iron—he would not let go.

As Mr. Townsend struggled, the professor turned and glanced helplessly at Fergie. "We've got a real problem on our hands, Byron!" he said. "Townsend has taken a nasty blow on the back of the head, and now he thinks he really *is* a Venetian admiral. I don't know what we are going to do, but we can't let him run off to his death. Thank God he brought the valise and the sword along—we might need them later on!"

Fergie looked into Mr. Townsend's eyes, and he saw that they were bleary. Under the rim of his hat was a sticky red mass of blood and hair. "Oh, great!" muttered Fergie disgustedly. "Just *great*! All we need right now is somebody who is out of his jug! Here comes John! I think the four of us are gonna catch it, but good!"

Johnny ran, huffing and puffing, up to the other three. When the professor explained the situation to him, he was silent. Something like panic was growing in his mind—were they going to get out of this alive? It didn't seem likely.

Suddenly in the distance a wild yelling began. Trumpets brayed and drums boomed. A great mob of turbaned soldiers was moving toward them across the grassy plain. Banners waved in the breeze, and the morning sun glittered on a forest of spears and cruel curved swords.

The professor's hand flew to his mouth. "Oh my God!" he gasped. "It's the Turkish army! They're *attacking*! And we can't go back to the well, because we're cut off! Come on, boys! We've got to reach the city walls before they do! It's our only chance! RUN!"

Letting go of Mr. Townsend's arm, the professor scooped up the sword and the valise. Then he began galloping madly toward the city walls. The boys pounded along behind him, but Mr. Townsend just stood there, glancing vaguely around, while the huge mob of soldiers got nearer. As he ran, Johnny looked behind him once or twice, but each time, he saw Mr. Townsend standing like a tree in the middle of the grassy field. On and on the three of them ran. They ran harder and faster than they had ever imagined they could, and the roaring army swept forward, a horrible human tidal wave. Like some huge object seen in a nightmare, the walls of Constantinople loomed closer and closer. All around them Johnny saw the wreckage left by the earlier attacks that the Turkish army had made—broken spears, an overturned wooden tower on wheels, and dead bodies. Mercifully Johnny did not have time to stop and stare at these things—he was too busy running for his life.

The three of them raced, while the frightful roaring of the soldiers got nearer and nearer. Once Johnny stumbled, but the professor immediately picked him up and hurried him on his way. If they reached a gate, would the people of Constantinople let them in, or would they think they were part of the attacking army? There was no time to think, only time to run, and as Johnny looked ahead through his fogged glasses, he saw another great wrecked siege tower. These tall wooden structures had been built so that the Turkish soldiers could climb up them and jump out onto the top of the city's walls. The defenders had sneaked out at night to burn this one, and it was just a mass of charred timbers. But why were they running toward it? Were they going to hide behind it? The professor was yelling to the boys, but his voice was lost in the loud noise that filled the air. Johnny saw a pit before him. He tried to stop, but the professor gave him a shove, and he went in headfirst, sliding and rolling down a long ramp of earth. Fergie came hurtling down after him, bumping Johnny to one side. Finally the professor jumped, bouncing along on his rear, with the sword in one hand and the valise in the other.

At the bottom of the pit Johnny closed his eyes and curled up into a ball. Any minute now soldiers would jump down into the pit and kill him. As he waited tensely, the yelling and braying of horns grew deafeningly loud, and then it died away. The army had gone on past.

"Holy H. Smoke!" sighed the professor as he wiped his forehead with his sleeve. "That was a close one! I thought those maniacs were going to turn us into chopped steak! Fortunately we found the entrance to a mine."

Johnny opened his eyes and sat up. They were squatting at the bottom of a deep shaft, but straight ahead the entrance to a low tunnel gaped. "Mine?" said Johnny in a puzzled tone. "What kind of mine?"

Fergie understood, and he grinned. "Oh, come on, John baby!" he said mockingly. "You've forgotten everything you ever read! This is one of those tunnels that they dig under the walls of a city during a siege. Then they stick in barrels of gunpowder and blow the wall sky high."

Johnny's fogged brain was slowly beginning to clear. "Oh . . . yeah," he said uncertainly. "Sure . . . I remember now. So what are we gonna do now? Hide down here till it gets dark again?"

The professor sighed and scratched the end of his nose. "We could do that," he said thoughtfully, "but it would be fairly risky. Sooner or later some Turkish soldier is going to come poking down this hole, and then good-bye to us! And even if that doesn't happen, we'd have to crawl back out and try to make our way past a lot of soldiers in order to get to the seacoast again. Even in the dark we might be spotted. And remember, we don't have a compass with us."

"Well, then, like John was saying, what are we gonna do?" asked Fergie grumpily. "Spend the rest of our lives down in this hole?"

The professor glared testily at Fergie. "No, we are not. I think we ought to see where this tunnel leads. If we get lucky, it might take us inside the walls of the city. From there we might find our way down to the docks and a ship that will take us back to Leander's Tower. And please don't get worried and think that I'll try to save the city with my flare gun—I just want to get us all back to Duston Heights in one piece!"

"That's a relief, I must say!" rasped Brewster, who had suddenly appeared in the darkness at the bottom of the pit. "This is definitely not a time for cheap heroics or daredevil stuff!"

"Thank you for your expert advice," growled the professor. "Would you care to lead the way?"

"I'll do what I can," said Brewster, "though it does seem to me that we have been spending a great deal of time underground."

They began to crawl down the low tunnel on their hands and knees. Brewster went first, casting a pinkish glow on the dank earthen walls. Then came the professor, shoving the satchel in front of him. Johnny clumped along next, with the professor's sword clutched awkwardly in one hand. Last came Fergie, with his switchblade knife held tight in his teeth. They crept on through the darkness, with only Brewster's pale glow for a guide. Finally they came to the place where the tunnel ended. It was a little room with dirt walls, a hollowed-out space where all of them could crouch together side by side. Overhead they saw the heavy foundation stones of a mighty wall. And in one corner stood three small wooden barrels. A small hole had been punched in the top of one, and a trail of black grains ran down the side of the barrel and across the dirt floor.

Johnny glanced nervously up at the heavy stones that seemed to hang perilously over his head. "Which wall do you think this is, professor?" he asked timidly.

The professor squinted. "I'd say it was the inner set of walls. They are the strongest and the thickest, and those stones up there are very, very thick. Hmm . . . I wonder why those barrels of gunpowder were never touched off? Maybe they lighted the trail of powder at the other end of the tunnel, and some dirt fell onto the powder halfway along and put out the fire. Well, I wonder if there is a way out of this end of the tunnel."

Taking the sword from Johnny, the professor hacked at the walls of the little room. In one place he found nothing but more dirt. But when he dug into the left-hand wall, the point of the sword struck something hard.

Working quickly the professor cleared a space about a foot wide, and the boys saw a row of smaller stones that were held in place by mortar. With his mouth screwed into a stubborn frown, the professor hacked at the mortar until one of the stones was ready to come out. He pulled at it, and it moved easily. The mortar was crumbly and old. Beyond the stone was blackness and a heavy smell of mold.

CHAPTER THIRTEEN

For several minutes the professor knelt there holding the stone he had pried out. It was about the size of a small loaf of bread, like all the stones in the wall. The pinkish glow cast by Brewster's magic light illuminated the professor's face, which showed that he was puzzled.

"So what is it, whiskers?" asked Brewster in his usual sarcastic tone. "Did you find an old tomb?"

"I was hoping that *you'd* have an answer for *me*," muttered the professor. "You always seem to know so much."

"You have an exaggerated idea of my knowledge," said Brewster sourly. "However, from the greenish gunk that is on one side of the stone you pulled out, I would say that you have broken into a water pipe of some sort. Perhaps—"

"Of *course*!" exclaimed the professor, snapping his fingers. "I remember now! There was an old water pipe here that ran from the aqueduct some emperor built. The pipe was replaced later when the walls were rebuilt during the reign of Theodosius II. If I am right, this pipe still runs down to a huge reservoir under the city walls. From there, maybe we can find our way up into the city."

"Not bad for an elderly crank," said Brewster. "Shall I go first and provide a little light?"

"Please do," said the professor. As the boys watched, the pinkish glow moved through the hole in the wall.

"P.U.!" exclaimed Brewster disgustedly. "It *stinks* in here! Are you sure you want to come in?"

"We *have* to!" said the professor. "Now kindly shut up while I do a little hacking."

Once again the professor jabbed at the mortar with the sword. Fergie helped as well as he could with his knife, and before long they were lifting another stone out, and then another, and yet another. At last there was a hole big enough for the professor to crawl through. He wriggled in, and Fergie came next. Last came Johnny, who was having trouble fighting down the panic that was rising inside him. He had always had a fear of being trapped in a small, shut-in space, and now that he had been in two underground tunnels in a short space of time, the fear had begun to grow. He had trouble breathing, and his heart was going like a triphammer. But he fought his feelings down and forced himself to follow the others into the foul-smelling pipe.

They crawled over slimy green stones. Far ahead Johnny could see the flickering pink glow of Brewster. For this he was very thankful. He thought of all the nightmares he had had about being buried alive, and he knew what he would feel like if he was in the dark. He could hear his breathing getting heavier and heavier, till it almost sounded like sobbing. Suddenly Fergie stopped and turned to glance back at him. "Are you okay, John baby?" he asked. He sounded worried.

Johnny had to swallow several times before he could talk. "I . . . I guess so," he said in a weak, throaty voice. "But I'm really scared, and I wish we were back home!"

"You and me both!" said Fergie firmly. "But don't worry—the prof and Brewster'll get us out okay. Let's go, before they get too far ahead of us."

Johnny pulled himself together and forced his arms and legs to move. He was scrambling forward again. But he hadn't gone very far when he heard the professor call out.

"Halt, everybody! We've got a problem! Low bridge ahead!"

Fergie and Johnny stopped crawling. Brewster's light was faint, but it was bright enough for Fergie to see what was wrong. Not far ahead a huge stone block had sunk down into the roof of the water pipe. The space that was left was just barely large enough for them to crawl through. Fergie felt a tightness in his throat. He had wriggled through a space like that once when he was cave exploring with some other boys. He hadn't enjoyed the experience much, but at least he had made it. But what would Johnny do now?

There was a long silence. Brewster's light got fainter, and then it grew again. Finally his familiar raspy voice could be heard, echoing weirdly in the tunnel.

"I have good news!" he said cheerfully. "After you crawl through the crevice you're home free! You come out onto a stone ledge above a lovely big reservoir. Hop to it, and you'll be through in no time!"

Johnny almost felt like cheering, but the sound stuck in his throat. He was much too scared to celebrate just yet. Grimly, one at a time, they began to slither through the crevice. The professor went first, and very soon he was on the other side, yelling encouragement to the boys.

"Come on, gentlemen!" he called. "You won't have any trouble at all! Wait till you see the size of this place! It's *enormous!*"

Fergie knew he was next, and he quickly got down on his belly. "Just do what I do, John baby," he whispered. "We'll be through in a jiffy."

Fergie began to wriggle along under the stone block like a snake. But when he was halfway through, Brewster called out in alarm. His voice sounded squeaky and thin.

"I'm sorry," he said, *"but I have to leave! I have been called back by the great god Thoth, and so—"* He never finished the sentence, and his voice faded to a far-off *Good-byyyyye* . . . that got fainter and fainter till it stopped. Brewster was gone, and they were in the dark.

"Drat!" roared the professor. "Hang on, everybody and I'll have a light for you presently." After a pause that seemed to last forever, the boys heard a *whcchh!* sound. And there at the far end of the crevice Fergie saw the professor, holding his Nimrod pipe lighter in his hand. "Hi there!" said the professor, grinning lopsidedly. "I'm Brewster's summer replacement. Not quite as old, perhaps, but twice as charming."

Eagerly Fergie scooted forward, and soon he was dropping down onto the stone ledge. Now it was Johnny's turn. Gasping and panting he struggled forward, while the professor held the lighter up to the mouth of the crevice and said encouraging things in a gentle, soothing voice. Johnny was in a terrible state. He kept imagining that the heavy stone block was coming down to crush him. Over and over he whispered every prayer he could think of. Finally, a few feet from the opening, he simply stopped.

"I . . . I can't go on," he said in a whimpering voice. "I . . . I have to go back, I really do."

"Nonsense!" snapped the professor. "You will do nothing of the kind! Give me your hand. *Do you hear me?"* The professor had stopped his mild-mannered coaxing, because he knew that it wasn't working, and became harsh and commanding, which was something he was better at. Johnny was startled; he jumped a bit and banged his head on the low stone roof of the crevice. But then he thrashed frantically forward and the professor grabbed his hand. The old man tugged mightily on Johnny's arm, and he managed to haul him through. When Johnny was safe, the professor sobbed and muttered incoherently as he hugged Johnny and said that he was sorry for being so nasty.

"It . . . . it's all right, professor," said Johnny. "I . . . . I know that you had to do it." Johnny was feeling pretty weepy himself, and he would have cried if Fergie hadn't been there. He hated to cry in front of Fergie, who was usually so controlled.

"*Well!*" said the professor as he let go of Johnny and turned around. "We are out of one mess, but we may be in another. Isn't this something?"

The steady flame of the Nimrod lighter illuminated a strange underground world. Beyond the narrow stone ledge stretched a huge water tank with a vaulted stone roof. Stone pillars supported the arches of the ceiling, and the black surface of the water glimmered faintly. How deep was the tank? How big was it? There was no way of telling.

As Johnny and Fergie stood staring in wonder, the professor walked quickly away and stooped. He picked up a piece of wood with a pitch-soaked rag wrapped around one end, and he lit it. "This lighter burns fuel like crazy," he said as he snapped the cylinder shut

"People must come down here occasionally. That's encouraging, I must say. Over there, if my eyes don't deceive me, is a boat. Come along, gentlemen—time's a-wasting!"

Johnny and Fergie turned to look where the professor was pointing. Sure enough, farther down the curving ledge, a rowboat lay on its side. Two oars were propped against it.

"I imagine that the Emperor's inspectors come down here now and then to check the water supply," said the professor as he bent over to examine the boat. "Hmm . . . it seems to be in pretty decent shape. The torch's flame is flickering a bit. There must be a draft blowing from somewhere across the water. There has to be a way out, and by the holy eternal powers, we are going to find it!"

The boys did not need much encouragement. They helped the professor heave the boat over onto its bottom. They threw the valise and sword into the stern, and then they carefully slid the boat down off the stone ledge into the water. While the professor and Fergie clung to the boat's prow to keep it from drifting away, Johnny jumped in. The boat rocked, but he settled himself quickly in the stern seat. By that time the other two were in the boat, and the professor was using one of the oars to shove them away from the ledge. Fergie sat in front and held the torch, which cast weird shimmering lights on the water.

"I have read about these reservoirs, but I never expected to see one," muttered the professor as he fitted the oars into the locks. "We will row in the direction of the draft and see what happens. In spite of Brewster's disappearance, I think we are going to be all right."

Bending his back the professor started to row. He hummed as he pulled at the oars, because rowing was a cheerful activity for him, and he remembered the time he had spent in a three-man scull at Princeton University. He maneuvered the boat in and out among the pillars. Black vastness hung all around them, and now and then a bat would flutter by. For a long while no one spoke. Johnny trailed his fingers in the water and watched the braided wake behind the boat. He felt gloomy, and he missed Brewster a lot.

"What do you think happened to Brewster?" he asked suddenly. His voice echoed strangely in this vast place, and the sound startled him.

"I wish I knew," muttered the professor. "He said something about being summoned by the god Thoth. Thoth is the Egyptian god of magic, and so I suppose he has power over a creature like Brewster. Maybe he will be back soon. But with him or without him we are going to get home safely—don't worry about that."

Johnny screwed his mouth into a tight frown. It was all very well for the professor to say "don't worry," but Johnny knew they were in a jam. They had to get back to Leander's Tower, but they seemed to be getting farther and farther away from the tower with every step that they took. And even if they arrived back there, they couldn't be sure that the Time Trolley would be waiting for them. Maybe it would take off by itself, the way it had when Mr. Townsend was running it. The three of them would be stuck forever in the year 1453, and they would probably end up as slaves when the Sultan's troops took the city of Constantinople. It was not a pleasant thing to think about.

The professor rowed, and the little boat nosed in and out past the tall, gloomy pillars. The torch that Fergie held went on flickering, and they steered in the direction of the draft. Soon the professor's cheerful humming died, and every now and then he put down the oars and held a wet finger up in the air to see if he could tell where the draft was coming from. Then he would pick up the oars and row grimly on. Johnny noticed that Fergie's torch was burning straight up—it wasn't wavering at all.

"Professor?" he asked in a tiny faltering voice. "How . . . how come the draft isn't blowing anymore?"

"I don't know," muttered the professor through clenched teeth. "There is something very odd going on in this place, but I don't know what . . ."

The professor's voice died. Out of the darkness straight ahead of them, a boat was drifting. It looked just like the one they were in, but it was empty. Or was it? The boat moved closer, and now it was alongside them. Johnny, Fergie, and the professor looked. There were three bodies lying slumped in the other boat. The bodies looked like the three of them, pale and cold and dead.

CHAPTER FOURTEEN

Fergie let out a loud yell, and he almost dropped his torch. Johnny closed his eyes and swallowed hard, and he started saying prayers under his breath.

"Angels and ministers of grace defend us!" breathed the professor. "What sort of devil magic is this?"

"I am the Guardian of the Sunken Palace," a loud, echoing voice said. "I was set up here in the time of the great Emperor Justinian. You must answer three questions if you expect to leave this place. Otherwise you will become like those in the boat near you. Are you prepared to answer?"

The professor was stunned, but he was determined to remain calm. "What sort of creature are you?" he asked warily. "And how is it that you speak English?"

"I am a magic stone head placed here to guard this place against those who might try to poison the waters," the voice replied. "I speak all languages on earth."

"Good God, *another* magic statue!" the professor whispered under his breath. "The woods are full of them, it seems!"

"Prof, what are we gonna do?" asked Fergie. "Can't we just row on past and forget about Whatsisface up there?"

The professor shook his head. "I'm afraid not. I have read about these magic Guardians before, and they mean what they say. We won't get out of here alive if we don't answer the questions. It's too bad Brewster isn't here to help us, but I know a lot of odd facts, and so do you and so does Johnny. Maybe we'll be able to outwit this vile creature."

"Are you ready?" the voice intoned solemnly. "I wish to begin."

The professor gritted his teeth and glared into the darkness. "All right," he growled. "What is your first question?"

"Name the Seven Kings of Rome."

Johnny's heart leaped. He had learned these names in Latin class last year, and he knew them as well as he knew anything. Proudly he rattled off the list, beginning with Romulus and Numa Pompilius, and ending up with Servius Tullius and Tarquin the Proud. After he had finished silence fell. The boat floating next to them drifted away and began bumping into one of the stone pillars.

"Very good," said the voice at last. "That is one question. Now for the second. Name the Seven Hills of Rome."

The professor turned to Johnny. "Well?" he whispered. "Do you know those?"

Johnny's brain raced. He had learned the names once for a Latin test, but could he dredge them all up again? "Quirinal, Viminal, Capitoline . . ." he began in a quavering voice.

"That is only three," said the voice nastily.

"Oh, give him a chance, for heaven's sake!" exclaimed the professor. "He's only just gotten started."

"Very well," said the voice. "Proceed."

Johnny glanced to his left, and to his horror he saw that the boat with the dead bodies in it was moving closer. His mind went blank. He could not have remembered his own name if someone had asked him what it was. Fergie was sitting at the other end of the boat, and he leaned forward to whisper in the professor's ear. Quickly the professor scrambled to Johnny's side.

"He says Palatine and Esquiline," the professor hissed anxiously.

"I heard that," the voice said pompously. "It does not matter who answers, so long as the reply is correct. Palatine and Esquiline are correct. That makes five. Two more are needed. Please proceed. A prompt answer would be appreciated."

The professor glared hatefully into the darkness. If this wretched stone head had a neck, he would gladly wring it. Two more . . . two more. Maybe he could help—after all, he had taught Roman history at one time. The professor's brain raced, and the other boat drifted closer and closer. An awful silence fell.

"Caelian and . . . and Aventine!" the professor screeched. "Am I right?"

"You are," the voice said in a bored tone. "And now there is but one question left. Name the present Emperor of Byzantium."

The professor grinned. This was a home-run pitch, thrown right across the middle of the plate. "Constantine XI Dragases Palaeologus," he said, rolling the name out grandly and triumphantly.

More silence. Would the stone head be satisfied? They waited tensely and tried not to look at the hideous thing that was floating on the water near them.

"You may pass," said the voice at last. "Thank you for your cooperation."

The boat that had been floating nearby vanished. Once again a cold breeze began to blow, making Fergie's torch flicker. With a deep, heartfelt sigh of relief, the professor picked up the oars and started rowing again. In silence they moved past more pillars, until at last they saw, up ahead, a broad flight of cracked marble steps that rose up out of the water. At the top of the steps a stout wooden door stood half open, and beyond it more steps could be seen. In a niche near the door stood an enormous stone head. With blank eyeballs it stared eerily out at them.

"That must be the thingamajig that gave us all that trouble," whispered Fergie.

"It is indeed," the head muttered, a trace of amusement in its voice. "Please have a nice day."

The boat drifted closer to the flight of stone steps. With a sudden lunge Fergie reached out and grabbed an iron ring that was bolted to the bottom step, and he pulled the boat tight against the landing. Nimbly the professor hopped out with the valise in his hand. Johnny threw the sword up onto the steps, and then he clambered out too. Fergie went last, as the other two held the boat close for him. As quickly as they could, they scrambled up the steps. The professor tugged at the door's iron handle, and with a lot of ominous creaking and groaning, it swung wide. The light of Fergie's torch showed the start of a winding stone staircase. They started climbing. The darkness gave way to faint daylight, and they began to hear noises—yelling and the clash of arms, and in the distance the booming of a great cannon.

"My lord!" gasped the professor as he paused and tried to catch his breath. "It doesn't sound good at all!" He struggled to the top of the stairs.

At last they came out into bright daylight in a room at the top of a tall stone tower. The tower was built into the inner line of the city's walls, and from its windows Johnny and the others could see a battle raging below them. The Sultan's great cannon had battered a wide hole in the outer walls, and through this gap thousands of soldiers were streaming in. The professor turned pale. He had read a lot about the siege of Constantinople, and he knew what was happening. This was the final attack. Before long the city would be in the hands of looting, angry, bloodthirsty men. Panicked, the professor led the boys out through an arch onto a broad walkway that ran along the top of the inner walls. Then the three of them stopped dead and stared in horror. Running along the wall toward them was a yelling mob of Turkish soldiers. And in the lead, waving a flashing sword, was Baltoghlu, their old enemy.

CHAPTER FIFTEEN

"Merciful heavens!" exclaimed the professor, putting his hand over his face. "I was hoping he was dead or in some other part of the battlefield. Ah well, if at first you don't succeed . . ."

The howling soldiers were getting closer. Baltoghlu saw the professor and the boys, and his eyes flashed angrily. This time there would be no mercy! As the boys watched in alarm, the professor calmly knelt down on the stone walkway. Digging his hand into the valise, he came up with a big cluster of Chinese firecrackers. Taking out his Nimrod lighter, he waited till the soldiers were only a few yards away. Then he lit the fuse and threw the firecrackers, which landed at Baltoghlu's feet. A long ripping string of small explosions filled the air, and clouds of acrid smoke rose. Then, while the soldiers wavered, the professor took his second weapon from the bag. It looked like a gray beer can with a lever on top. Quickly he released the catch and threw the tear-gas bomb. As clouds of eye-watering smoke shot from the little can, he snatched up his valise and yelled to the boys, who stood cowering in the doorway of the tower room.

"That ought to take care of them for a while!" the professor roared triumphantly. "Come on! There's a staircase over there, and it leads down to the ground. We've got to run while there's time!"

They clattered down the stone steps and ran madly away from the city walls. Behind them the loud frightening noise of battle went on. When they had run as far as they could, they threw themselves down behind a hedge that grew near a dusty little road. The professor squinted up at the sky. Then he smiled and turned to the boys.

"Relax, gentlemen!" he said. "As far as I can tell, it's only a little past noon, and the Turks won't be able to smash their way through the defenders until about four in the afternoon. I was panicked when I saw all those soldiers pouring through that gap in the walls, but I remember the details of the siege quite clearly, and I'm sure I'm right."

Fergie glanced sourly at the professor. "Well, whoopy-doo for your memory!" he said. "So what about old Balto-whosis, the guy with only one eye and a lousy temper? There were a lot of soldiers with him, weren't there?"

The professor smiled confidently. "You needn't worry about Baltoghlu and his friends," he said. "They are due to be trapped and wiped out by some of the Emperor's soldiers. You see? If you read history you know what's going to happen . . . or rather, you know what happened at one time."

Johnny sighed wearily and mopped his forehead with his sleeve. "Professor?" he said. "How are we gonna get something to eat? I feel like I'm starving to death."

"Say no more!" exclaimed the professor, holding up his hand imperiously. Digging his hand into the battered old leather satchel, the professor came up with a box of Mounds bars. He handed one to each boy, and they tore into them greedily. It had been a long time since they had had anything to eat.

"Nothing like chocolate for quick energy," muttered the professor as he wolfed down a Mounds bar. "Mmm . . . good! Now then, kiddies, we had better be up and going. From the position of the sun, I would say northeast is off that way. If we travel in that direction, we should run into the Great Middle Way, which runs straight through the heart of the city to the Church of the Holy Wisdom. Then—"

"Hey, wait a minute!" snapped Fergie. "Are you tryin' to tell us that you're gonna use the flare gun inside the church? Do you mean you've changed your mind *again*?"

The professor sighed wearily and nodded. "I'm afraid

so, Byron. The idea may seem idiotic to you, but it may be our only chance. It is much later than I thought. The city is surrounded. At this point we can't get a ship to take us to Leander's Tower. We might have done it a few days ago, but not now. We have to scare the soldiers of the Sultan into thinking that an Angel of Light has descended among them. If we can do that, we might just possibly get back home safe and sound."

Johnny munched another candy bar and glanced at Fergie. The look on his friend's face showed how they both felt—they were filled with despair. The professor's plan seemed just as wacky as it ever had, and they were sure it would fail. But they had to go to the church with him. If there was one chance in a million that his plan would succeed, they had to take it. There was no other choice.

After they had finished eating, they set off to find the Great Middle Way. They hiked through a field of weeds and an apple orchard. They passed a street of ruined stone houses whose windows stared out blankly at them, like the eyeholes of skulls. The little rutty cart track they were on was grass grown and deserted. Johnny and Fergie felt as if they were out in the country, instead of being in the heart of a great city. The professor pointed out that Constantinople had once been a bustling, crowded place, but in 1453 it was already half deserted. At last they came to a wide road paved with cobblestones.

"How far is it from here to the church?" asked Fergie.

"About two miles," said the professor. "You two have gone on ten- and fifteen-mile hikes in the Boy Scouts, so it shouldn't seem difficult. We'd better get moving if we're going to get to the church before the Sultan's soldiers do."

The three of them tramped down the wide, deserted road. In the distance they heard church bells ringing, and far behind them the sounds of the battle that was raging at the city walls. Once a group of soldiers went thundering by on horseback, raising clouds of yellow dust. Steadily, grimly, they hiked. They passed through the Forum of Theodosius, a broad open area full of statues and temples. No one was there. The people of Constantinople were either on the walls fighting or in the churches praying. At last they saw the great domed Church of the Holy Wisdom before them. A strange droning sound rose from it. It was the sound of worshipers chanting, praying desperately for the safety of their city. Fergie and Johnny looked up in awe. They had read about the siege in books, and they had seen pictures of the church. And here they were—scared half to death.

For a long time they just stood in the middle of the road and stared at the church. The professor heaved a weary sigh and mopped his face with his sleeve.

"Lord love a duck!" he groaned. "Now I know why

the Romans had flat feet—they wore sandals all the time! My own feet feel as if they were being roasted over a fire, and my legs feel like rubber. Ah well, at least we're here! We had better head for the church. The sun is low in the sky, and that means that before long—"

The professor's voice died. He turned and looked down the long road, into the glare of the setting sun. From the distance came a sound like a football crowd on a Saturday afternoon—only this sound was more savage, and filled with shrill, bloodthirsty screeching.

"Oh, Lord!" gasped the professor. "It's the Turks! They've broken through, and they're coming! Come on, boys! *RUN!*"

Hiking up the skirts of his robe, the professor ran frantically toward the front door of the church. Fergie pounded along beside him with the satchel, and Johnny ran with the sword over his shoulder. Closer and closer loomed the church, and they could see that men were struggling to close the tall bronze doors. "*No! No! Wait for us!*" yelled Johnny, and they ran faster. The men who were closing the doors stopped and stared at the three strange figures that were galloping toward them. The professor racked his brains, trying to find something he could say. Brewster was not here to translate, so he had to try to speak Greek. The professor had studied classical Greek in college, and he could say a few things in it. As he raced past the startled doorkeepers, he yelled, "*We are here to save you!*" in Greek.

The men gaped, but they held the doors till all three were inside. Then they pulled the heavy bronze slabs inward till they shut with a loud, ominous *boom*. The professor and the boys were inside, but the enemy was at the gates.

CHAPTER SIXTEEN

Inside the Church of the Holy Wisdom, a large crowd of people milled around. Most looked frightened, and many were on their knees, crossing themselves over and over and praying tearfully. Far overhead the vast dome loomed, and the red light of late afternoon slanted in through many small windows. Under the dome was the altar, and at it three priests in heavy, gold-colored robes chanted the service of vespers, the evening prayer of the Byzantine church. Countless candles and oil lamps burned in the gathering darkness, and the smell of incense hung in the air.

As quietly as possible the professor and the two boys made their way forward through the crowd. Some stared in wonder at the clothing of the two boys, but most were too filled with fear to notice what was going on around them. The professor glanced nervously around as he walked, and he felt despair growing inside him. For the first time he realized how silly and hopeless his plan was. It had seemed reasonable when he was sitting at home thinking about it, but it did not seem reasonable now. The chances of his plan working were just about zero. He and the boys would either be slaughtered or end up as slaves of the Turks.

With cheerful thoughts like these running through his mind, the professor elbowed his way past the praying people. He had to make it to the high altar before the Turks got in. Outside the great bronze gates they were bellowing like beasts, and thunderous crashes rang out. *Boommmm! BOOOMMMM!* A heavy log was hitting the doors, over and over. With the boys at his side the professor had reached the open space in front of the altar. *BOOOMMMM! BOOOMMMM!* The log struck the doors again, and with an ear-shattering crash the doors fell. The soldiers of the Sultan rushed in and at that moment the professor grabbed the valise from Fergie, dashed past the startled priests, and leaped onto the altar.

"*Turn, demons, turn!*" he roared as he jammed a flare into the wide muzzle of the gun. "*I am an Angel of Light, and your doom has come!*" For a second the vast mob of soldiers paused in the doorway of the church. Then they started forward, and the professor closed his eyes, raised the gun, and fired it into the air. The fizzing flare shot up and burst just under the roof of the dome. A blinding flash of white light filled the air, and everyone in the church fell to the floor as if struck dead. Fergie and Johnny had closed their eyes just before the professor fired. They opened them. The Turkish soldiers were gone. The acrid smell of gunpowder drifted through the air, and for a moment all was silent. The people in the church got to their feet, and they started cheering. The professor stood there stunned for several seconds, and then he grinned and bowed. But just as he was stuffing the flare gun back into the valise, he heard a noise that he had dreaded. The Turkish soldiers had recovered, and they were coming back.

The professor was beside himself with rage and fear. He had a couple of flares left, but they would only postpone the moment of doom. "I should have known," he muttered to himself as he reloaded the flare gun. Just then he heard a *pinggg!* near his right shoulder, and a familiar raspy voice said, "Greetings! And what sort of idiotic mess have you gotten yourself into *this* time?"

The professor didn't know whether to rant or cheer. "Brewster!" he spluttered. "Where . . . Look, there's no time to talk. You can see what's happening! *Do* something!"

"I'll give it a try," said Brewster calmly. "Shall I do the big fancy once-in-a-thousand-years thing I told you about earlier?"

"*Yes, yes, for God's sake YES!*" yelled the professor at the top of his voice. "*DO SOMETHING! PLEASE!*"

"Very well," said Brewster.

The soldiers were pouring back into the church. Suddenly a loud voice filled the air. It was Brewster saying a spell in ancient Egyptian. An enormous black falcon appeared. Its head touched the top of the dome, and its outspread wings brushed the sides of the church. In a thunderous baritone it sang:

The bear went over the mountain
The bear went over the mountain
The bear went over the mountain
To see what he could see!

For a second the soldiers hesitated. Then they turned and fled, shrieking in terror. The black falcon disappeared. The professor stood on the altar, looking bewildered but very pleased. Hastily he stuffed the flare pistol back into his valise, and then he bowed like an actor taking a curtain call. This time the applause and cheering were even greater than before. Amid the shouting Johnny recognized the only Greek word he knew: Nikē!, which means "Victory!"

As the joyful noise died down, the professor climbed off the altar and made his way back to the boys, who were still pounding their hands together, tears streaming down their cheeks. The crowd parted for them as they walked solemnly and slowly toward the front door of the great church. And a disturbing thought occurred to the professor.

"Do you think this really is victory?" he whispered to the boys. "What about the other Turkish soldiers who got inside the town? They won't flee just because of what happened in here, will they?"

"They most certainly will *not*!" said Brewster, cutting in rudely. "And as for the soldiers who just ran out of the church, they'll be back once they've recovered their wits. As I've said before, you have a very exaggerated idea of my powers. We have time to save ourselves, but that's about all. The city is doomed."

The professor was thunderstruck. What were they going to do? He felt sorry for the poor people in the church, but he felt sorriest for himself and the boys. Turks were pouring into the city through the land and sea gates. The slaughter and looting would begin, and there was not much that he or anyone could do about it. Their one hope was to get the Tabergan, but it was with the nasty monk, and he was God knew where—dead probably, or on a boat to a safe port. The professor felt total despair, worse then any he had felt since this adventure began. Through his incompetence he had led the boys into a trap from which there was no exit.

Fergie and Johnny stood staring at the professor in dismay. They had heard Brewster's words, and they felt sick terror in their stomachs. Nevertheless, they were willing to give it one more try.

"Come on, prof!" said Fergie, tugging gently at the old man's arm. "We might be licked, but I think we oughta go down fightin'! Which way is that gate with the lighthouse? We can try to get there. Come on!"

Fergie shook the professor's arm harder, and at last

he snapped out of his trance. Glancing around wildly he saw the gaunt ruins of the Hippodrome rising in the distance. If they walked a little to the left of the Hippodrome, they would be going in the right direction.

"Okay, boys!" he said with a wild gleam in his eye. "Here goes the last of the Childermasses!" With a flourish he handed the satchel to Fergie and took the Knights of Columbus sword from Johnny. Drawing the tarnished blade the professor started running down a narrow street that he hoped would lead him to the Gate of the Lighthouse. The boys ran with him. They had not gone far when they saw the small cobblestoned square that lay before the church of the Hodegitria. There a crowd of angry men pushed and shoved. Two soldiers held a struggling man in a red cape—Mr. Townsend, of all people! The white-faced monk stood before him, waving a small object that he clutched between thumb and forefinger. It looked like a fountain pen.

"Now!" rasped the monk as he shoved his face closer to Mr. Townsend's. "Tell me what *this* is. It is not a quill pen or a stylus, but some devilish pen that I have never seen before. Why were you carrying it? What did you intend to do with it? *Answer me!*"

Astounded, the boys and the professor paused at the entrance to the square. The monk and the soldiers had not noticed them yet, but they would pretty soon. After a quick glance at his two friends, the professor made up his mind. With a loud, bloodcurdling yell, he dashed forward, waving the sword high above his head.

"Princeton Tigers, go go GO!" he screeched, and he bore down on the monk with murder in his eye.

The monk was startled at first, but he pulled himself together quickly. Snatching a short-handled spear from a soldier, he braced himself to meet the professor's attack. The Knights of Columbus sword swung down in a glittering arc, but it wasn't really meant for fighting, and the blade broke in two when it hit the stout spear handle. With a scornful sneer on his face the monk lowered his spear and moved in for the kill. Immediately the professor went into a crouch and shuffled warily forward. He had been taking a mail-order course in jujitsu, and he tried to remember some of the tricks he had learned. The monk was puzzled. He had never seen an unarmed person try to fight an armed one before. Cautiously he jabbed with the spear at the short, snarling figure dancing around him. Once, twice, three times the monk tried, but each time the professor ducked nimbly aside. At last the monk thought he had him, but just as he made his thrust, the professor ducked in under his outstretched arm, grabbed the monk, picked him up, and threw him down hard on the ground. The professor jumped on top of the monk, scrabbling frantically at the drawstring of a leather pouch that hung from the monk's belt. He grabbed the Tabergan, and with a joyful screech he leaped to his feet and began running back toward the boys, who were still cowering at the edge of the square. Suddenly he stopped. He had forgotten about Mr. Townsend!

But just as he turned, he saw a fearful sight. A band of Turkish sailors had landed at the Gate of the Lighthouse, and they were streaming in, yelling and waving weapons. The soldiers who were guarding Mr. Townsend decided that they had seen enough. They let their captive go and ran. Breathlessly the professor dashed up to the old inventor. Did he still think he was an admiral of Venice? To the professor's great relief his friend's eyes were clear, and he gave him a warm welcoming smile.

"Not bad, old boy!" he exclaimed, grinning. "But what do we do now?"

"Come with me," yelled the professor, who could see the sailors getting closer every second. "Come on! RUN!"

The two men dashed back to where Johnny and Fergie were waiting. Quickly the professor rattled out his directions—everybody had to lock elbows, with himself in the middle. The Turkish sailors charged, but the professor calmly took the Tabergan in his hands and cried, "*Go where I say, Tabergo, Tabergan!*" Then he twisted the magic handle. In the same loud, clear voice he told the Tabergan, "*Take us to Leander's Tower!*" He twisted it again. A rock thrown by one of the sailors hit the professor's shoulder, but a split second later the two men and the two boys were soaring up over the square, and over the city walls and the choppy waters of the Sea of Marmara. The flight was even scarier than the earlier one had been. Mercifully it ended, and with a jarring *thump!* all four were dropped onto a little spit of sand that stood outside the entrance to the tower. Anxiously the professor glanced around to see if everyone was all right. They were, and Johnny had even managed to bring the professor's valise with him. The light of late afternoon cast bloody splashes on the walls of the tower, and the travelers thought sadly of the things that were going on in the doomed city across the water. Then silently they began to climb the worn steps that led to the top floor of the tower. As they stomped along behind the two men, the boys wore anxious frowns. They remembered what Mr. Townsend had said about the unpredictable behavior of the trolley, and they wondered if it would still be there.

At the top of the stairs the professor glanced quickly to the right. Was the veil there? He'd soon find out. Quickly the professor fished his pipe tamper out of the leather bag that hung round his neck, and when he touched the wall with it, the veil parted. The four entered the trolley, which smelled like a dusty, shut-up attic.

"Ahhh!" Mr. Townsend breathed, raising his arms gratefully. "It's *so* great to be back! Now, folks, if you'll just take your seats, I'll have us back in Duston Heights in a jiffy."

The professor glowered at Mr. Townsend, but he managed to fight down his anger. "My dear sir," he said in his coldest and most formal tone, "don't you think it would be better if *I* handled the controls? I managed to make several trips in this machine without having anything bad happen, and I am confident that I can get us home safely in double-quick time."

Mr. Townsend stiffened. "Are you implying that I am not capable of controlling the machine that I *built myself*?" he asked.

Johnny and Fergie glanced nervously at each other. "Uh . . . folks?" Fergie put in with a weak smile. "Do you . . . well, d'ya think maybe you could flip a coin or do somethin' like that?"

This was the wrong thing to say. The two men gave Fergie dirty looks and went back to glaring at each other. They argued for a while, but finally the professor heaved a resigned sigh and stepped aside. For once in his life he was going to be cooperative. "Very well," he said, waving his hand toward the control panel. "Go to it, my friend!"

The boys sat down in the back, and the professor plunked himself down on a fold-out jump seat at the front of the trolley. Mr. Townsend took his place in front of the control panel. He set dials and shoved levers. Since he was seated nearby, the professor could not resist watching, and what he saw horrified him. Mr. Townsend was a real fumblefingers, and he kept accidentally hitting knobs and levers after he had set them. Then he had to go back and reset the controls, and this put him into a foul temper, so his blunders got worse and worse. Meanwhile a loud excited hum rose from the trolley's motor, and the air began to shiver and grow warm. The professor began to wonder if he ought to say something, and he was just opening his mouth to make strangled sounds when Mr. Townsend impatiently shoved a lever forward. With a sickening lurch the trolley jumped backward, throwing the professor and the boys out of their seats. The trolley roared in reverse, bumping and hiccuping like a small plane fighting its way through air pockets until it came to a screeching halt, and the passengers were once again pitched about on the trolley's floor. Mr. Townsend was thrown from the control seat, and he landed on top of the professor. Little wisps of smoke came curling out of the trolley's control panel. A smell of burned electrical insulation filled the air. Where they were, nobody knew.

CHAPTER SEVENTEEN

Groaning weakly Mr. Townsend picked himself up. "Oh, dear . . . oh, dear . . ." he moaned as he tottered down the aisle. "I can't imagine what happened. Where do you suppose we are?"

The professor glanced grimly at the windows, which were lit with a sullen red glow. "I guess we'd better find out," he said quietly. "The rest of you follow me, and be careful."

Fearfully Mr. Townsend, Johnny, and Fergie lined up behind the professor, who took the pipe tamper from its leather bag and pulled the handle that opened the folding doors. At a touch from the tamper the blue veil parted, and the four travelers stepped out of the trolley one by one. They found that they were standing on the tiny sandy island where Leander's Tower had once stood. But the tower was gone. So was the Sea of Marmara—its bed was just a deep, undulating valley full of sand and shells and the ribs of wrecked ships. Across the way, where Constantinople had once stood, rose the shattered ruins of a modern city. Twisted masses of girders stretched spindly arms into the sky. These were the skeletons of skyscrapers that had been wrecked by some hideous explosion. The city seemed to be abandoned, and the dusky red air had a sulfurous taste. In the coppery sky, ghostly and enormous, hung the moon. It loomed impossibly close to the earth, and its craters and mountain ranges could all be seen clearly.

The professor said nothing. He knew that they were looking at some scene out of the far-distant future. Twenty-fifth century, thirtieth century—who could tell? Silently they filed back into the trolley, and the door hissed shut. Without a word Mr. Townsend knelt down and opened a sliding door under one of the trolley's seats. He pulled out a tool kit and went to the front of the car, where he knelt down again and began unscrewing the metal plate that covered the control panel. Behind the plate lay a confusing mass of wires, cams, springs, winking Christmas-tree bulbs, rods, and vacuum tubes with glowing filaments. One of the tubes was dark, and Mr. Townsend jerked it from its socket. When he inserted a new one from his kit, the tube glowed, and with a relieved sigh he began screwing the plate back on. Finally he stood up and wiped his forehead with his sleeve.

"I think it'll run all right now," he said as he turned to the professor, a sad, apologetic frown on his face. "The fault was mine, all mine. I should never have manhandled the controls that way. I always get upset when someone is looking over my shoulder. Perhaps you had better run this thing."

The professor patted Mr. Townsend on the arm and took his place in front of the controls. He set the PLACE dial for Duston Heights, and the DATE and TIME dials for the day their journey had begun. Then, holding his breath, the professor turned the starting lever to ON, and the trolley began to hum and tremble. After a brief hesitation it leaped forward, back into the past, back to the 1950's. The car hurtled on, rattling and swaying from side to side. Finally it screeched to a halt, and immediately the professor jumped up. He rushed to the side door, pulled the lever, and parted the veil. Then he let out a loud joyful exclamation. They were back in the dank stone tunnel where their journey had begun. With his valise in his hand the professor clumped down the iron steps to the ground. Johnny and Fergie followed quickly. Mr. Townsend glanced about in a confused way, and then he gasped in surprise.

"Good heavens!" he said. "You've unblocked the archway—the one that leads back to the basement of my house. Why ever did you do that?"

The professor looked astonished. "Why did I . . ." he began in a wondering tone. "Heavens, man! How else could I have gotten to use your wretched trolley? Do you think . . ." The professor's voice trailed off, because it had just occurred to him that Mr. Townsend's question meant that the tunnel had been blocked up when he had zoomed off into the past thirty years ago. Unless he had sealed it up on the day he left—which did not seem likely—how had he gotten from his house to the trolley?

Mr. Townsend stood watching the professor with his arms folded and a smug smile on his face. "Let me enlighten you. Come on—right this way," he said.

The professor and the boys followed Mr. Townsend up a short flight of cement steps to the subway platform. They watched in amazement as the old inventor reached into the ticket booth and spun the ticket roll three times, counterclockwise. From deep down under the platform came a slow grinding of gears and a clatter of chains. Slowly the ticket booth began to swing off center, revealing a manhole-sized opening. Cleated iron steps wound down into darkness.

"A secret passage!" breathed the professor joyfully. He could hardly contain his delight. "I've *always* wanted to have one in my house, and now . . . But tell me—where does it go?"

Mr. Townsend smirked. "Follow me, folks, and you'll find out. But be careful—there isn't any handrail."

Mr. Townsend carefully picked his way down the

spiraling stairs, and the others followed. At the bottom a level passage stretched away into pitchy blackness. The professor quickly fetched his Nimrod lighter out of the valise, and a spear of yellow flame leaped up, lighting the tunnel. Once again Mr. Townsend took the lead. After about fifty yards, they came to a flight of wooden steps that led up inside the walls of the professor's house, and they started climbing. Finally Mr. Townsend slid back a wooden door, and they all stepped into a tiny room that the professor knew well. It was his fuss closet. It was a private place in the professor's study where he went to rant and pound on the walls when he was in a foul mood. For this reason the little room was padded with gym mats, and on the inside of the closet door hung a sign that read, TO FUSS IS HUMAN: TO RANT, DIVINE!

"What on earth *is* all this?" asked Mr. Townsend wonderingly as he looked at the padded walls.

The professor was embarrassed. He could feel his face growing red. "Oh . . . uh, well, it's, er, sort of a practical joke. I'll explain it to you sometime. Come on downstairs to the kitchen, and we'll have something to drink. It's *great* to be home!"

The others agreed, and they followed the professor through the study and down the front staircase to the kitchen. Johnny and Fergie got a couple of Cokes from the refrigerator, and the two men had small glasses of Irish whiskey. After rummaging around in his kitchen cupboard, the professor dug out a box of black-and-gold

Balkan Sobranie cigarettes. With a courteous bow he offered one to Mr. Townsend.

"I've been trying to give up smoking," said the professor as he lit both cigarettes and blew clouds of smoke into the air. "However . . . ah well, we all have our weaknesses. Aaah, it is so *wonderful* to be home!" He leaned back in his chair, sighed, and then let out a loud exclamation. He had just noticed the kitchen clock.

"Good gravy!" he exclaimed. "Is it really only a few minutes after the time when we took off on this trip? The clock says nine thirty, and the windows are dark, so . . ."

"It's no coincidence," said Mr. Townsend with a strange smile. "If you set the dials for the time you left, that's when you get back. The laws of time are suspended for time travelers: Hasn't it occurred to you that I ought to be a lot older than I am? I disappeared thirty-one years ago, and I was in my fifties then. Do I look like an eighty-year-old man? Do I *act* like one?"

The professor was stunned. A lot of things had been happening, so he had never really spent much time thinking about Mr. Townsend's age. But now that the subject was brought up . . .

The professor squinted owlishly at Mr. Townsend. "Heavenly days, McGee!" he exclaimed. "Do you mean to say that you haven't grown old *at all* while you were bumming around outside of Constantinople?"

"Bumming around, indeed!" Mr. Townsend said, laughing. "I aged a *little.* Not thirty-one years, but a bit." He paused and frowned sadly. "But I'm sure I was declared legally dead long ago, and what money I had must have gone to my sister, who lives in Maine. I wonder if she's still living. If she is, I'll go up and stay with her. If it turns out she's dead, perhaps you can take me on another trolley ride and drop me off somewhere in America in the not-too-distant past. I might be able to earn a living predicting things that I know are going to happen."

"Well, all you need to do for the time being is rest," said the professor as he refilled Mr. Townsend's glass. "You're welcome to stay here as long as you like—this was your house, after all." He paused and puffed at his cigarette. Then suddenly he threw a sharp glance at Mr. Townsend. "If you don't mind my asking," he said, tapping his friend on the chest with his finger, "how did you get inside the city in the middle of the siege? That must have taken some doing!"

Mr. Townsend shrugged. "Not really," he said. "I don't remember everything, but I think I got knocked down by a soldier outside the walls of Constantinople. When I woke up, I found that my head was bloody, and I couldn't remember how I had gotten into this field outside the walls!"

"That was the second blow," put in the professor with a grin. "When I met you out in that field earlier in the day, you already had a head wound, and you thought you were an admiral of Venice. You wouldn't let me help you. That second knock must have come when those soldiers went by. We were sure that you had been killed by them."

Mr. Townsend smiled. "Luckily, I wasn't. I just picked myself up and walked into the city, through one of the holes that the cannon had made in the walls. Then I wandered around looking for you and the boys, but that insane monk got his hooks on me. All in all, I think we're very lucky to be alive!"

The professor nodded and sipped thoughtfully from his whiskey glass. Mr. Townsend's attention turned to the black valise, which had been dumped on the floor next to the kitchen table. Reaching down he fumbled about and came up with the flare gun. Its muzzle was blackened, and when Mr. Townsend sniffed, he noticed the acrid odor of freshly exploded gunpowder.

"Good heavens!" he exclaimed. "What on earth have you been doing? I know that you used a flare on that Turkish galley that my ship captured. But that was some time ago. It seems you were shooting flares again. Why?"

The professor coughed in an embarrassed way. "It's a long story," he said. "I'll tell it to you sometime. I was just trying to change the course of history, but it seems that there is some evil genie in the universe that won't allow you to do things like that."

"A good thing too!" said Mr. Townsend emphatically. "I mean, if people started fiddling with the past, maybe they would fix it so you and I didn't exist. Then where would we be?"

The professor thought about this, and then he and

Mr. Townsend got into a long boring discussion about time. Meanwhile Fergie and Johnny had finished their Cokes, and they were thinking about going home. On the trip back in the Time Trolley they had been cooking up all sorts of fancy explanations to tell their families to explain their long absence. But now they realized that they hadn't been gone long enough to need explanations. Fergie left first. He mumbled a few polite things and ducked out the back door, slamming it behind him. When Johnny decided to go, the professor followed him to the front door. They paused on the porch to sniff the air of the chilly April evening. As Johnny was starting down the front steps, a thought occurred to him. "Oh my gosh!" he said as his hand flew to his mouth. "I forgot all about Brewster! You don't think we left him behind accidentally, do you?"

The professor shook his head and laughed. "Not a chance!" he said. "Gods of Upper and Lower Egypt know how to take care of themselves. I suspect that he'll be sitting on my desk when I go to bed tonight. For all I know he may be here right now, hovering invisibly. He likes to do things like that." He paused and glanced up at the empty air. "Brewster?" he asked. "Are you there?"

No answer.

"Blasted overrated hunk of stone!" the professor growled good-naturedly. "He's *never* around when you want him!"

CHAPTER EIGHTEEN

When Johnny got back to his grandparents' house that night, they had no idea that he had been on a dangerous journey through time and space. He drank a cup of cocoa in the kitchen, and his gramma told him that he'd better hurry up and get to bed, because there was school in the morning. Fergie called Johnny on the phone later that night, and the two of them had a brief conversation about the wild things that had happened to them. Already the Constantinople adventure had begun to seem like something they had dreamed about, and yet they knew that it was real.

Weeks passed, and it began to look as if Mr. Townsend would be staying at the professor's house for a long time. Mr. Townsend's sister was dead, and there really wasn't anywhere else he could go—unless he took another trip into the past with the Time Trolley. So the professor bought Mr. Townsend some modern clothes, and tried to make him feel at home in the 1950's. This was hard, because Mr. Townsend had never heard of Willie Mays, Marilyn Monroe, or automatic shift cars. He said more than once that he felt like a fish out of water, and it was clear to everyone that he was not very happy.

During the first week of May the professor decided to throw a party. This was surprising because he didn't entertain very much, and he always did a lousy job of it when he tried to be a genial, fun-loving host. Nevertheless, plans for the party got under way: The professor sent invitations to all his friends, and he went to a local store and bought a big supply of balloons, party favors, and paper plates. Saturday night, the sixth of May, arrived, and so did the guests: Gramma, Grampa, Fergie, Johnny, Mr. Townsend, and Dr. Charles Coote. The professor had ordered plates of cold meat, delicious *hors d'oeuvres*, and soft drinks, and he had champagne and cognac for the grown-ups. It was a nice party, but everyone wondered. Why was the professor throwing this big blowout? As they gobbled food and sipped soda pop, Fergie and Johnny tried to question the professor, but he just smiled blandly. It was all pretty strange.

Around nine thirty Gramma and Grampa went home. The rest of the partygoers gathered upstairs in the professor's study, and he uncorked a bottle of fifty-year-old

Napoleon brandy. Everybody got some, even the boys, and then the professor proposed a toast:

"To our safe return," he said solemnly. He clinked glasses with everyone, and they drank.

"I think Professor Childermass ought to be congratulated for his quick thinking and his courage," said Mr. Townsend as he refilled his glass. "He really saved the day for all of us, and I'd like to add that—"

"I think you are forgetting someone," said Brewster, who had noiselessly appeared on the corner of the desk. "I had a small part in the victory, as you may recall."

The professor glanced at Brewster over the top of his glasses. "I might have known you'd show up to take credit," he said, smiling wryly. "All right, all right—you deserve ninety percent of the credit, to be fair. We apologize for leaving you out, and we salute you. If you hadn't done your big-bird routine, the boys, Mr. Townsend, and I would be in a slave camp somewhere."

"Thank you," rasped Brewster. "Now that I have been given proper credit for my heroic actions, I shall depart. See you in the funny papers." With a faint *plip!* like a soap bubble popping, Brewster vanished.

"Amazing creature," muttered Dr. Coote as he stared at the place where Brewster had been a second before. "It's hard to believe that he's real!"

"Oh, he's not real at all," said Mr. Townsend placidly. "He's just an illusion whipped up by our wonderful friend the professor. I wish I could do tricks like that!"

The professor gazed at Mr. Townsend in despair. He had tried to convince his friend that Brewster was real, but it was like talking to a stone wall. Finally, reluctantly, he had given up. After a long sip of brandy the professor *harrumph*ed, as he always did when he was going to say something important. "Folks," he said loudly, "I have an announcement to make—or rather, my friend Al Townsend has one."

Mr. Townsend coughed nervously and put his glass down on the professor's desk. "I want to tell you, first of all," he said, "that I have enjoyed the professor's hospitality—he is a kind and generous person, and I won't forget what he's done for me. However, I really feel uncomfortable here in the middle of the twentieth century. All my friends and relatives are dead, and I feel . . . well, useless and out of place. So I'm going to use the trolley to go back to Topsfield, Massachusetts, in 1896. The professor has managed to buy some old-fashioned clothes for me at a costume shop, and I have two suitcases packed and ready to go."

Dr. Coote was astonished. "Good heavens!" he exclaimed. "Topsfield is a lovely little town and all, but . . . well, what are you going to *do* there in the Gay Nineties?"

Mr. Townsend smiled mischievously. "I'm going to set myself up as a mystic and general all-purpose foreteller of the future. After all, I know about a lot of the things that have happened since 1896. I can predict Queen Victoria's death and President McKinley's assassination. I know about the stock-market crashes and wars and who won the American and National League pennants. Before long I'll be rich and famous. You can read about me—in old books and newspapers, of course."

Johnny and Fergie looked at each other in alarm. They really didn't know what to say. Was it possible that Mr. Townsend knew about their secret midnight expedition to Topsfield? If he didn't know, then how had he happened to choose the year they had? It really was too much of a coincidence to be believed. After giving each other a few more nervous looks, they turned to the professor, who was eyeing them strangely and making little *hem! hem!* noises in his throat.

"I have something to add to what Al has told you," the professor said solemnly. "He wanted me to take him in the Time Trolley, but I'm going to let him take the blasted piece of tin and keep it. If it was sitting in my basement, I'd be tempted to use it, and then God knows what would happen! We just barely made it back from Constantinople by the skin of our teeth, and I just don't want to take any more silly chances."

Johnny, Fergie, and Dr. Coote all murmured their approval. Later, while the others waited, Mr. Townsend changed into an 1890's-style outfit. When he came back, everyone gathered around the door to the professor's fuss closet. For old time's sake, Mr. Townsend wanted to take the secret passage back to the subway tunnel.

One by one the guests clumped down the rickety wooden staircase. At last everyone stood waiting outside the rear door of the trolley. Mr. Townsend's suitcases were safely inside, and the machine was humming and vibrating. The professor stepped forward and pumped Mr. Townsend's hand vigorously.

"Good-bye and good luck, my friend," he said. "And if you happen to run into my grandfather, tell him to avoid horseback riding—he died at the age of ninety-eight when a horse threw him."

After a final wave Mr. Townsend climbed up the iron steps and disappeared into the trolley. The steady hum of the trolley's engine rose to an ear-splitting whine, and the air around the trolley began to waver. Then, with a sudden *whoosh*, the machine shot forward and disappeared. For a long time everyone was silent. Finally Johnny spoke up.

"Gee, I hope everything works out okay for him," he said with a worried frown. "Did he take any money with him?"

The professor smiled. "Oh, yes—he has about a thousand dollars in old coins and banknotes. I got them at a rare coin shop in Boston. In 1896 a thousand dollars will go a long, long way. And he can always come back here." He paused and turned to Johnny and Fergie. "By the way," he said, smiling innocently, "do you think he'll run into the ghosts of you two running around Topsfield in the winter of '96?"

Johnny and Fergie were flabbergasted. Then they stared at the ground, and their faces slowly turned red. How on earth had the professor found out?

The professor laughed, and so did Dr. Coote—they had known about the boys' secret for some time, and they had just been waiting for a chance to surprise them. When the laughter died down, the professor put his arm around Johnny and smiled warmly. "My boy," he said, "there are a lot of things in this world that you don't know—and that goes for you too, Byron. For one thing, when you set the time-machine dials for a certain place and time, the iron pointers inside the dashboard make marks on the paper-covered drums that have the list of times and places. When Mr. Townsend took off the dashboard to replace that burnt-out tube, he noticed that Topsfield and the date December 5, 1896, had been marked. But he had never gone to Topsfield, and neither had I. That left the possibility that someone else had been fooling around with the Trolley. And that someone eats Clark bars. There was a wadded-up wrapper from one in the waste can next to the driver's seat. And it is a well-known fact that you, Byron, have a passion for Clark bars. So, gentlemen? Was it fun?"

Fergie grimaced. "It sort of was," he muttered. "Whyn't we go upstairs an' finish the cake, an' we'll tell you all about it."

After another quick glance at the empty trolley tracks, the two boys and the two old men started walking slowly up the dank brick tunnel that led back to the professor's basement. All of a sudden Johnny halted. There was one more loose end, something he had forgotten about till now.

"Hey!" he said. "Professor, what happened to the weird gadget with the handle? You know, the Tabergan. Do you still have it?"

The professor smiled calmly. "No, I left it on a window ledge in Leander's Tower. I imagine those ghostly knights will come and get it back, or else it will return to them automatically."

Fergie looked exasperated. "Prof!" he exclaimed. "Are you out of your jug? That widget coulda made us millions of dollars! Everybody wants something that will carry them all over the world just like that, zippity-zoo! We could've cleaned up!"

"Maybe," sighed the professor as he kicked a little stone down the tunnel. "But I felt the Tabergan belonged to the knights. Besides, I hated the way I felt whenever the thing took me anywhere. I got all shaken up and sick to my stomach."

"Isn't that odd, Roderick," Dr. Coote put in sarcastically. "That's just the way I feel when I ride with you in your car. I'm sorry I didn't get a chance to try the Tabergan, because I might have preferred it to—"

With a wild yell the professor leaped at his friend and tried to put his neck and arms in a full-Nelson grip. But Dr. Coote broke free and dashed off down the tunnel, while the boys stared after them and laughed.

John Bellairs is the critically acclaimed, best-selling author of many Gothic novels, including *The Curse of the Blue Figurine*; *The Mummy, the Will, and the Crypt*; *The Lamp from the Warlock's Tomb*; *The Spell of the Sorcerer's Skull*; and the novels starring Lewis Barnavelt, Rose Rita Pottinger, and Mrs. Zimmermann: *The House With a Clock in Its Walls*; *The Figure in the Shadows*; *The Letter, the Witch, and the Ring*; and *The Ghost in the Mirror*. John Bellairs died in 1991.